HENRY REED'S JOURNEY

HENRY REED'S JOURNEY

BY KEITH ROBERTSON
ILLUSTRATED BY ROBERT McCLOSKEY

A YEARLING BOOK

Published by
Dell Publishing
a division of
The Bantam Doubleday Dell Publishing Group, Inc.
666 Fifth Avenue
New York, New York 10103

The trademark Yearling® is registered in the U.S. Patent
and Trademark Office
ISBN: 0-440-43555-2
This edition published by arrangement with The Viking Press, Inc.
Printed in the United States of America

February 1974

10

CW

To all Henry's Kansas friends
who made him feel so welcome

HENRY REED'S JOURNEY

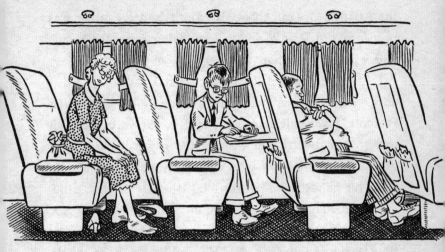

Tuesday, June 15th—En route to San Francisco

My name is Henry Harris Reed and this is my journal. It is my private property and in case it gets lost, please return it to me in care of my uncle, Mr. J. Alfred Harris, RD 1, Grover's Corner, Princeton, N.J. I'll send you whatever you spend in postage. It's very important that I get it back as I am going to make it into a book and publish it.

First I guess I'd better explain how I happen to be flying to San Francisco. My father is in the diplomatic service. Last summer we were living in Naples, and I flew to the United States and spent the summer with my Uncle Al and Aunt Mabel in Grover's Corner, New Jersey. I had a lot of fun, and I guess my aunt and uncle didn't mind having me too much, because they invited me back again this summer. This time, however, I am not crossing

9

the Atlantic Ocean. About six months ago my father was transferred to Manila, and so I am flying across the Pacific and will arrive in San Francisco.

Last year I kept a journal of what I did and used it as a report when school opened. I got an "A" on it. Miss Prescott, my English teacher, said it was very good, although she did complain about the pages being sort of grimy. She says anyone who keeps a journal should always wash his hands before writing in it just as he should before meals. That's silly. Can you imagine Robinson Crusoe going down to the stream and washing his hands every time he wrote in his journal? He would have been caught by the cannibals long before he finished his book. Probably what upset Miss Prescott was the angleworm that got pressed between pages 42 and 43. I remember using a worm as a marker, but I wouldn't have closed the notebook on it. I wonder if Midge could have done that? That's the sort of trick she'd think was hilarious.

Midge Glass was my partner in a research business in Grover's Corner last summer. She was the only person under forty living there, so I didn't have much choice. However, she turned out to be a good sport and very smart, even if she is a girl. We got to be very good friends. Midge doesn't giggle, and giggling is the main thing wrong with most girls.

Mr. Glass is a research chemist, and he is attending a convention in San Francisco. Midge and Mrs. Glass are with him, and they are all going to drive back to New

Jersey. The trip is their vacation. Since I was due to arrive in San Francisco at the same time they planned to be there, I was invited to drive back with them. That was a lucky break for me, and I am looking forward to the trip. I've been all over Europe and part of Asia, but I haven't seen much of the United States. I guess New York City, New Jersey, and Washington, D.C. about cover my travels. Also it seems that whenever I go any place I go by plane. You get on a plane, eat lunch, look at a few midget houses if it's clear and at clouds if it isn't, and then it's time to get off. Traveling by car will be a wonderful change. My father says one of the reasons he is sending me back for two summers is that he understands the younger generation in the United States is learning a new language and it would be nice if I learned it, too, so I could understand my own countrymen. He's probably kidding. He's referring to words like "cool" and "square" which everyone knows no matter where he lives.

Traveling by car all the way across the continent from San Francisco to Princeton, New Jersey, will be fun. Before I left Manila I went to the library and got out all the travel books I could find. They were a pretty sorry lot. Americans write dozens of guidebooks to Africa and Europe and Tibet, but they don't write about the United States. The best I could find were a few books that gave the mileage between towns and told you what the best roads were. Some of the books told about the best hotels and motels and recommended restaurants. I guess facts like those are helpful, but none of the guidebooks had any of the really important information that someone my age needs when he is crossing the country. After about three days of reading, I could see that there is a crying need for a topnotch travel book about the United States. Whoever writes the first one will probably make a fortune. I am going to keep this journal, and when the trip is over I'm going to edit it and publish it. When you look at my book you'll find what you want to know, not just the names of restaurants, motels and museums. It will tell what states sell firecrackers, where the best rodeos are held and when, where there's good fishing, what to use for bait, where the amusement parks are located, where you can get good root beer, and whether the natives of the different towns are friendly or hostile.

Right now I'm flying over the Pacific Ocean, quite a few hours from San Francisco. There's not too much to say about the Pacific except that there's no excuse for an ocean being so big. I read somewhere that three-fourths of the earth's surface is covered with water. With all that water I can't see why fish chase each other around eating one another. There's plenty of room, and most of it is in the Pacific Ocean. We're up about ten thousand feet, and as long as the fish and the ocean stay where they are and we stay where we are, I guess I shouldn't kick. I'd like to see some land, though—particularly San Francisco.

Wednesday, June 16th — San Francisco

I arrived in San Francisco this morning, and I am staying at the Hotel Carlton where they are having the convention of research chemists. Midge and her mother met me at the airport. I didn't recognize Midge standing beside the gate, because she was all dressed up in a dress instead of being in the shorts or slacks she wore last summer. She is a trifle taller, a little scrawnier, and has a few more freckles, but otherwise she is just the same. She is still wearing her hair in a pony tail, and she bounces up and down like a tennis ball when she's excited.

I didn't think she would know me, because I've grown a lot and look much older and more experienced. She did though.

"Hey, Marco Polo!" she yelled at the top of her voice, jumping up and down. "Welcome to sunny California!"

What she said didn't make sense, because it was raining, and of course my name isn't Marco. I'm used to Midge and know that half the time what she says isn't supposed to mean anything. Women aren't so hard to understand once you realize that.

I wasn't long getting through customs, and a few minutes later we were on our way to the hotel. The convention is to last another day, so I unpacked when I got to my room. I had presents for Mrs. Glass and Midge that my mother bought in Manila. It wasn't their birthday, but my mother say it's polite to give people presents when they are going to take you all the way across the country. I had another present for Midge, but Mother wouldn't let me bring it. It was a shrunken head that came from New Guinea, a very fine specimen, and I'm certain Midge would have liked it. Instead Mother got some hammered Indian jewelry. I guess Mrs. Glass and Midge like it, judging from the way they squealed when they opened it. I'll bet Midge would really have squealed if she'd opened a package with a shrunken head.

We got to the hotel a short while before noon. This afternoon was pretty dull. Mr. Glass attended meetings with all the other chemists, and Mrs. Glass went somewhere to have her hair done. There was no sign that the rain would stop so there wasn't much to do but hang around the hotel. Midge and I went down to the lobby and wandered around looking at the shops for a while. Then we each bought a book and sat down in the lobby to read. After half an hour or so the rain turned to a damp drizzle.

"It doesn't look too awful," I said. "Maybe we could walk over to Chinatown."

We had a guidebook with a map in it, and, according to that, Chinatown began only a few blocks from the hotel.

"I think we'd better ask first," Midge said. "Dad and Mom wouldn't like it if we wandered off and got lost."

"How are we going to do that?" I asked. "Your dad's got meetings all afternoon, and your mother is out being re-decorated."

"We'll get permission from Dad. There's a coffee break about every hour and a half. We can go sit outside the hall and read there. Then we'll catch him when he comes out."

The meetings were being held in a small auditorium on the ground floor. Outside the auditorium there is an ante-room like the lobby of a movie theater. A man came out as we arrived and said that we had just missed a fifteen-minute break but that two papers were being read which weren't too long and there would be another intermission in about forty-five minutes. It was quieter in the little reception room than out in the main lobby, so we sat down on the sofa in the corner and began to read. We had just found our places when a tall, thin woman with a high, silly orange hat hurried in. Trotting behind her without a leash was a miniature French poodle. Poodles look ridiculous naturally, and this one was carrying a woman's shoe in its mouth.

"Oh, hello there," the woman said to Midge. "You don't happen to know if Professor Atkins has started his paper on amino acids or not, do you?"

"I don't know who Professor Atkins is," Midge said. "There's a man with a white goatee and a shiny, bald head talking now."

"That would be Mr. Durfee," the woman said. "That's good, Professor Atkins must be next."

"Your dog has somebody's shoe," I told her, trying to be helpful.

"Yes," she said, without even glancing at the dog. "Amy always has a shoe. All my friends give her their old shoes. She has more shoes than I do. She's forever hiding them in the strangest places."

Amy wagged her entire rear half, put the shoe down in front of Midge, and then lay down contentedly.

"She likes you," the woman said. "How long are you going to be here, Margaret?"

"Until they come out," Midge replied. For a moment I didn't know who the woman was talking to, because I'd forgotten that Midge's real name is Margaret.

"Would you mind keeping an eye on Amy?" the woman asked. "I'd take her inside, but I'm afraid that she'd be bored with amino acids."

"Sure," Midge answered. "Have you got a leash?"

"You won't need one. Just let her wander around. As long as she doesn't go out in the main lobby she'll be all right." She turned to the little dog and spoke to her just as she had been speaking to Midge. "You can stay here with Margaret, Amy. I'll be right in there. Be a good girl."

The dog seemed to understand, because she jumped up on the sofa between Midge and me and sat down. The woman then turned and went into the auditorium.

"Who was that?" I asked.

"I think her name is Allison," Midge said. "She is supposed to be a brilliant food chemist. She lives in

16

Philadelphia and has been up to our house several times. The dog is always with her and always has a shoe."

I petted Amy a minute, but she didn't pay much attention. Both Midge and I went back to reading. A couple of minutes later we looked up, and the dog was gone. She had disappeared without a sound. I looked at the floor, and her shoe was gone too. The door to the corridor was closed, and no one had been in or out, so I knew she couldn't have gone very far. I nudged Midge and pointed to the door into the lecture hall. It was ajar.

"I guess Amy went in to hear about amino acids after all," I said.

"She won't disturb anyone," Midge said. "She's always quiet. Almost never barks." With that she buried her nose in her book again.

Several minutes later I glanced up, and there came Amy trotting through the door of the auditorium, a shoe in her mouth. She came across to where we were and disappeared behind the sofa. The sofa was placed across the corner, and there was enough room behind it for six poodles. If she preferred to stay back there in privacy, it was all right with me. However, she didn't stay long. When I glanced up as I turned the next page of my book, she was just disappearing through the door into the auditorium again.

I came to a really exciting part of my book, and I didn't pay too much attention to Amy for the next fifteen or twenty minutes. No one else came in, and there was no way she could wander off, so neither Midge nor I figured

she needed much watching. I had a vague impression that she was busily trotting back and forth, but as Midge had said, she was a quiet dog. I came to the end of the chapter and looked up. There was Amy coming back again, her shoe in her mouth as usual.

"She'll wear out the carpet with all her trotting back and forth," I said to Midge. "Look at her, she's as busy as a nursery-school teacher."

"French poodles always are," Midge replied. She looked at the dog and then down at her book. Suddenly she looked up again. "Say, something is wrong here. That isn't the same shoe."

"Here, Amy," I called. "Let me see your shoe."

The dog trotted over and deposited the shoe in front of

me. It was a dark-blue shoe with a small bow on it. I hadn't noticed it closely before, and for all I could tell, it was the same one. Midge didn't think so, however.

"The other one was black and had a lot higher heel," she said positively. "It didn't look a bit like this one."

"Where would she get a different shoe?" I asked. "She hasn't left the place."

"In there," Midge answered, nodding her head at the auditorium. "There are quite a few women chemists in there. Women always wear shoes that are too tight, especially when they're at some affair like this. Someone has taken off her shoe, and Amy has traded with her." Midge began laughing. "I'd like to see the woman's face when the lecture's over and she starts to slip her shoes on again. Amy's shoe is much smaller than this one. Whoever it is will think her feet are swollen."

"I guess the thing to do is to hold on to this until we find out whose it is," I said, leaning down to pick up the shoe.

I put the shoe on the sofa; Amy jumped up beside it and promptly went to sleep. Five minutes later the lecture ended, and people began to file out. They congregated in the lobby in small groups talking and smoking cigarettes. I picked up Amy so she wouldn't slip away, and Midge carried the shoe. People were still straggling out slowly, but we managed to slip into the auditorium. We thought that whoever owned the shoe would be inside looking for it and we wouldn't have much trouble locating her. It wasn't that easy. There must have been a hundred and fifty people altogether, and sixty or so were still inside. There were little knots of two or three here and there, talking about chemistry, I suppose. There were a number of women, and many of them were either still seated or looking around with funny expressions on their faces.

"I guess we'll have to announce it," I said. "Why don't you get up on the seat and ask who is missing a shoe?"

"Good idea," Midge said. She kicked off her own shoes and stood on one of the seats. She held the shoe high in the air. "Is anyone here missing a shoe?" she called.

It was noisy, and she had to repeat her question in a louder voice. There was a sudden silence. Finally, after a pause, about fifteen women all answered at once. Almost every woman there was looking for a shoe.

The whole place was immediately in an uproar. It seems that Amy had been much busier than we had suspected. Women all over the auditorium were standing on one foot. They may have been brilliant chemists, but they certainly were baffled by the simple little problem of losing a shoe. If it hadn't been for Midge and me, they'd have been hours getting things straightened out. All that was needed was a little system. Actually, it was the same as an Easter-egg hunt except that we were hunting shoes. The women who were missing shoes didn't help much; they stood around helplessly on one foot, or if they were missing both shoes, they sat around and glared. I guess chemists are too dignified to go barefooted.

Amy had done a thorough job. She had collected every

loose shoe she could locate. She took some out to the lobby and hid them and hid others inside. Doctor Allison realized what had happened and took charge.

"May I have everyone's attention please," she called. "It seems my dog Amy has been up to some of her tricks and has hidden some shoes. If the gentlemen, who still have the use of both feet, will assist, I am certain we can locate all the shoes in a few minutes."

The men thought the situation was hilarious, and they spent more time laughing and making remarks than hunting. They didn't make the women any happier when they did locate a shoe, because they would hold it up and announce the size. I think they even stretched things, because I've never heard of so many size tens and elevens. I know one thing about women chemists—some of them haven't much of a sense of humor.

Midge and I found more shoes than all the rest put together. We located five in back of the sofa alone. Altogether it didn't take much longer than ten minutes to get everyone shod again. One man suggested that they have shoe breaks in the future instead of coffee breaks, and another wanted to present Amy with a medal for adding a little excitement to the meeting.

We finally located Mr. Glass, and he said that we could walk over to Chinatown. "It will be safer as far as we here are concerned," he said. "I don't know how the Chinese will feel about it though. Your Uncle Al predicted things like this."

I knew right away what Mr. Glass meant. My Uncle Al claims that there is a special sign of the zodiac called the sign of the Great Auk and that once every thirty years or so in a leap year a few people are born under this sign. Both my mother and I were born during leap year, and Uncle Al says we are Great Auk people. According to him, strange things happen when we are around. The stars get all mixed up and so does everything else. Of course he's just kidding, and I think he made up the whole story. Nowadays people with any common sense don't believe in astrology. Also, I asked several people who said they knew a lot about astrology, and they said they never heard of the sign of the Great Auk. I'm surprised that Mr. Glass paid any attention to Uncle Al. A scientist like Mr. Glass knows that astrology is just superstition. Besides, nothing really happened today except that little mix-up with the shoes, and Amy is not my dog, so that can't be blamed on me.

When we got to the front entrance of the hotel it was raining again, so we didn't go to Chinatown after all. There was a movie down the street, and we went to that instead. Maybe we'll get to Chinatown tomorrow.

This evening I told Midge about my plan of keeping a journal of our trip and then publishing a travel book. She thinks it's a good idea. She wants to write in it too, but I don't think much of that. According to her the travel book would be more popular if it also had a woman's point of view. I don't want to get it filled up with a lot of stuff about clothes and hairdos. Besides Midge would give a tomboy's point of view instead of a woman's, anyhow.

"That will fit right in with an idea I had for our firm," she said after I told her about the journal.

"What's that?"

"We'll collect something interesting from every place we visit—a curio or something special from the spot or maybe something historic. Then when we get home we'll set up a travel museum in the barn and charge admission."

It isn't a bad idea at all. Of course I don't think it's as good as mine, but still it's good. You see, my mother and father own a lot down the street from Uncle Al in Grover's Corner, New Jersey. There's nothing on the lot except a barn right near the road. Midge and I had our research firm there last summer. If we could get together a good collection and put up a big sign, we might make quite a bit of money. I could sell copies of my travel book at the same time.

Thursday, June 17th—San Francisco

If this entry is scrawled and hard to read it's because I hurt my wrist today, and it isn't very easy to write. I'll explain how it happened later.

Mr. Glass had meetings and lectures again all day today, and Mrs. Glass went over to Oakland to have lunch with an old schoolmate. They didn't know what to do with us, so they finally agreed it was all right for us to go visit Fisherman's Wharf. I'm not a bit worried about being able to look after myself in a strange city. I've been all over the world, and I managed to get across both the Atlantic and the Pacific by myself. It isn't very hard to find your way around. All you have to do is ask someone for directions. It's funny but a lot of adults don't like to do that.

There is a cable car that goes almost all the way to Fisherman's Wharf. We walked down Powell Street to Market,

where there is a turntable. They turn the cars around on this and start them back up the hill. The cars are funny little stubby cars with some seats that face forward and some that face sideways. The sides are open, and there is a long running board that runs the full length of the car. People hop on and off and hang on like flies.

The car is pulled along by a steel cable that runs under the ground. A man in the center of the car operates a big

lever that grips the cable and makes the car move. It's very unusual, and whoever invented the system must have been a smart engineer.

The car was practically empty when we got on. I stood up on the open side but the conductor wouldn't let Midge stand beside me. She was furious and said she was going to send the streetcar company a copy of the Nineteenth Amendment.

We rode for several blocks, the only ones on our side of the car. Midge was sitting in one of the side seats facing outward, and I was standing up, right in front of her. Then a woman carrying a parakeet in a small cage got on and sat down beside Midge. The parakeet was a beautiful bright blue, and he seemed to be having a wonderful time.

The woman saw that both Midge and I were interested in the parakeet, and she asked, "Do you like parakeets?"

"I had a white one once," I told her.

"They're pretty, but I think I like the common green parakeet best of all. I have more of those than any other color."

"How many parakeets do you have?" Midge asked.

"Fifteen. I like parakeets."

There wasn't much question about that. She must also like noise, because fifteen parakeets can make quite a racket.

"Where are you taking him?" Midge asked, nodding toward the blue parakeet.

26

"Just out. Amos has never been to Fisherman's Wharf, and it was such a nice day I thought he'd enjoy the trip. It was his turn."

"His turn for what?" Midge asked.

"To go out. Whenever it's nice and I'm going someplace that I can carry a cage conveniently, I take one of my pets along. They're caged up all the time, and I think they enjoy seeing the world and having a little change of scene as much as we do."

I wish my father could have been there to hear that speech. He claims that my mother and I are completely crazy on the subject of animals and birds. At least I've never taken any of my pets for a cable-car ride.

"We're going to Fisherman's Wharf too," Midge said. "We're just visiting San Francisco."

"Where are you and your brother staying?"

Midge didn't bother explaining that we weren't brother and sister; she simply said we were at the Hotel Carlton. I didn't hear much more of the conversation because people began getting on in droves. So many hopped on the running board that I got forced down several places until I wasn't standing in front of Midge any more. All the seats were soon taken, and the step seemed filled to me, but somehow more people crowded on at every stop. Finally, about two-thirds of the way up the hill an enormous fat man got on right beside me. I didn't see how there could possibly be room, but he managed to find some. He got his feet on the step, grabbed the bar, and then wiggled his stomach until finally he forced his way in between me and a tall, thin man to my right.

There was a big six-foot, husky man on my left who looked as though he lifted weights for a living. There I was, squeezed between the weight-lifter and this big fat man. We went about three blocks during which I got about two chances to breathe. Then the big fat man turned to look at something, and his big stomach turned with him. What happened to me was the same thing that happens when you take a wet watermelon seed and squeeze it between your thumb and forefinger. I was squeezed right off the car and popped out into the street. I landed on my behind on the pavement, and before I really knew what was happening the car was too far away to catch. I could hear Midge shouting, "Henry! Henry! What's happened to you?"

I landed with quite a bump. It would have been worse except that I half caught myself with my right hand. That's how I hurt it and why I'm having so much trouble writing. Naturally I landed in one of the dirtiest spots on the street, and the whole seat of my pants was covered with a big dirty smudge that I couldn't brush off.

The car was moving slowly, but my fall shook most of the breath out of me, and I didn't feel like running. Besides, running up the hills in San Francisco is something only a monkey could do. I started walking after the car, wondering how I would find Midge, when I saw her get off at the stop a block ahead.

Midge was so mad you would think she was the one who had been squeezed off.

"I told him what I thought of him!" she said. "I wish I'd had Wolfie Gannet's teeth."

"Who's Wolfie Gannet?"

"A kid in our school who has sharp teeth like a wolf. I'd have bitten that man right in his fat stomach!"

We had to wait about five minutes until the next car came along. It wasn't so crowded, and we both got seats. We rode to the end of the line and then walked the few blocks to Fisherman's Wharf. This was very interesting, but I was disappointed. I saw more tourists than fish, and there were more restaurants than fishing boats. We walked around for a while, and then Midge noticed a big building that advertised "Oriental Goods and Exotic Imports" at bargain prices. Naturally she wanted to go shopping, and since I didn't have anything else to suggest, I agreed.

I was glad we had gone after I got inside. It was an enormous building and was operated like a big discount center. You wandered around with a basket, helping yourself. They sold everything, ranging from carved Chinese figures to Indian brass trays. There were all sorts of rugs, mats, bamboo blinds, and thousands of other imports. I guess they had everything except firecrackers. Midge bought a birthday present for her mother and a present to take home to her grandmother.

I saw quite a few things I would have liked, but since I will have to fly back to the Philippine Islands at the end of the summer, I knew I couldn't buy anything big or heavy. Then I happened to wander into the food department. It was filled with wonderful things—fried grasshoppers, chocolate-covered ants, canned rattlesnake meat, and smoked lizards. I got a can of the ants and a can of the grasshoppers. I'm going to take them to school as part of my lunch next fall. I'll bet that will cause a stir, especially if Miss Prescott, our English teacher, sees them. She's the finicky type.

I moved on to the Italian delicacies and had picked up a can of Parmesan cheese, two small cans of tomato paste, and a package of hot pepper seeds when Midge appeared.

"What are you going to do, make spaghetti?" she asked, thinking she was being funny.

That was exactly what I planned to do. Midge wouldn't believe me at first. My mother learned how to make good spaghetti sauce while we lived in Naples. It's the best in the world—even better than the Neapolitans make. My Aunt Mabel's spaghetti is about the worst, even worse than that you get in a can. She knows it too, and last summer she told me to be certain to learn the recipe and to come back and teach her. She'll be amazed when she finds out I remembered and have some of the most important ingredients.

We took our stuff to the check-out counter. By the time we left the store it was noon. We went back to Fisherman's Wharf and were trying to decide where to eat when we met the woman with the parakeet.

"I see you found your brother," she said to Midge.

After Midge had finished saying what she thought of the fat man, we asked the woman to recommend someplace where we could get some good sea food.

"There are dozens of places that serve sea food, and most of them are good. If you don't want an entire meal but something light like clams on the half-shell, a shrimp salad, or an Alaskan king crab, come with me. I have a favorite place. It isn't much to look at, but the food is good and quite reasonable."

That appealed to me, because my money has to last all the way across the United States, and no matter what happens I'm going to save some to buy fireworks when I find them.

She took us to a small place where you sit at a counter. There were only three empty seats, two together and then another, one seat away. The woman took the one empty seat and put her parakeet on the floor beside the stool. Midge and I took the two stools together.

"You get an enormous shrimp cocktail, if you like shrimp. It's the specialty of the house," our friend said.

Both Midge and I took her advice and ordered the shrimp cocktail. The service was fast, and in less than two minutes they put a huge plate of shrimp in front of each of us. It was all arranged in a ring on lettuce with a big bowl of cocktail sauce in the center.

"Is that horse-radish?" Midge asked, pointing to a glass container in front of me. "I like red-hot cocktail sauce."

I passed her the horse-radish, and then I thought of my hot pepper seeds. I picked up my bag from the floor and found the package.

"Try some of these if you want something hot," I said, opening the box and handing it to Midge. "Don't use many though, because they'll burn your tongue off."

Midge took a shrimp, dipped it in cocktail sauce, and then sprinkled a few seeds on it. She put it in her mouth, began chewing, and then reached for her glass of water.

"Boy! Are those things hot! I'll stick to horse-radish, thank you!"

The man on the stool between Midge and our friend with the parakeet finished and got up. The waiter came over and started to clear away the dishes.

"Let's slide over one," Midge suggested.

Before we had a chance to move, the big fat man who had squeezed me off the car came bustling in, just as he had on the cable car, and shoved in between Midge and the parakeet woman. He overflowed the top of the stool so far that it disappeared from sight. He plunked both elbows on the counter, the right one almost in Midge's plate. Both Midge and the woman had to move over to the edges of their stools to make room for him.

The waiter was still clearing away the counter, but the fat man didn't wait. He barked out an order for a shrimp cocktail. In no time at all the waiter was back with the shrimp, and in even less time, the man had gulped it down. He leaned on the counter and practically shoveled his food into his mouth. We were half through when he sat down, but he still finished ahead of both Midge and me. There must have been twelve or fourteen enormous shrimp per plate, but he was an enormous man, and I suppose they were just a taste for him. We were so full that we even hesitated before ordering any dessert. Then I ordered pie, and Midge decided on ice cream. While we were ordering, the fat man interrupted to order another shrimp cocktail. I don't think they expect people to have elegant manners at a lunch counter, but our waiter seemed to expect at least a few. He gave the man a withering look and said, "Yes sir! Coming up!"

The fat man got up from his stool and went over to the cigarette machine. While he was gone the waiter brought our dessert and the second plate of shrimp. He put the shrimp in front of Midge and her ice cream at the fat man's place. I didn't pay too much attention to what Midge was doing except that I know that she switched plates, because a minute later she was half finished.

"Let's hurry up and get out of here," she said. "I don't want to get crushed again."

The fat man couldn't find the right change for his cigarettes and had to go to the cashier. He got back to the counter just as Midge got up. He sat down, dunked a giant shrimp in the cocktail sauce, leaned over, and shoved it in his mouth. It was an enormous mouthful. He began to chew, and then, as we picked up our packages and started toward the cashier, he seemed to explode. He spat out a big mouthful of half-chewed shrimp all over the counter top, making an awful mess. He gave a bellow that sounded like a sick water buffalo and began to choke and cough. He waved his arms around like a crazy man, spilling his glass of water into what was left of his shrimp.

He hopped off his stool faster than I imagined anyone of his size could move. His legs were spread apart as he hopped, and his left foot landed on the parakeet cage, which was on the floor beneath the stool to his left. This threw him off balance and wrecked the cage. A big, husky man was walking by and whether he was trying to catch the

man or was just protecting himself from being crushed, I don't know. He kept the man from landing with too much of a thud, but even so, the whole building shook.

The fat man sat on the floor quivering, gasping, and bellowing, with everyone looking at him. I thought he'd had a fit. Midge didn't seem to be interested.

"Let's go," she said.

"I'd like to see what's wrong with that wounded hippopotamus."

"He's just got a stomach-ache from eating like a pig," Midge said. "Let's get out before he shakes the building down."

I didn't want to leave, but I paid the cashier and followed Midge to the door. As we reached it, there was new excitement. The parakeet woman began to screech, pointing up at the light fixture above the counter.

"Amos!" she yelled. "Amos is loose. That big lout wrecked Amos's cage. Somebody help me catch Amos!"

I suppose Midge and I were the only ones who knew who Amos was, but several others finally noticed the parakeet. No one volunteered to help, though. The management was too busy with the fat man. Both of the countermen and the manager were grouped around him. He still sat on the floor coughing, wheezing, choking, and sputtering. He hadn't managed to say anything intelligible except "water." One waitress hurried to get a glass of water.

"If I stand on the counter, I think I can reach Amos," I told Midge.

"Somebody else will catch him," she said. "We'd better hurry."

That wasn't like Midge. She usually wants to be right in the middle of any excitement, and I couldn't think of any reason we should be in a hurry. I borrowed a newspaper from someone and put it on the counter. I like animals and birds, and usually they like me. If you move slowly you have much better luck catching anything than if you grab. I put my hand up gradually, and Amos sat quietly. He was probably scared half out of his wits by all the fuss the fat man was making. I got him with the first try.

I got down and handed him to the parakeet woman, who began cooing and fussing over him. I picked up the cage and tried to bend it back into shape, though this bothered my hurt wrist. Meanwhile they had managed to get the hippo back on his feet, and he had regained his voice somewhat. He was still half choking, but from what I could understand, he was accusing the restaurant of trying to poison him.

"Let's go outside where there isn't so much racket," Midge suggested. "Amos will be less upset."

"Yes, let's get out before that fool wrecks something else," the woman agreed.

We all went outside and across the street, where we found a bench. I worked on the cage for about five minutes and finally fixed it so that it would hold Amos again. The woman put him inside, and I fastened the door shut with a piece of string. It took us five minutes more to get away, she was so grateful. She must have thanked us five times.

"Now, where are you in such a hurry to go?" I asked.

"Back to the store," Midge said.

"What for?" I asked. It was only one o'clock, and the store didn't close until six. I didn't expect to spend the next five hours shopping.

"I want to get a box of pepper seeds," Midge said.

I knew right away from the expression on her face what she had done. "How many did you use?" I asked.

"About a third of the box," she said. "I just dumped them in and gave the cocktail sauce a quick stir. I'll buy you a new box."

"No you won't. It was worth it," I told her. "I'm going to take the cost out of the money I have put aside for firecrackers. Not even a firecracker could have caused an explosion like that one."

Saturday, June 19th—Yosemite National Park

I'm writing this in Yosemite National Park. It's the most beautiful spot I've ever seen in my life. The mountains are the equal of any in Switzerland, and of course no other country in the world has anything like the redwood trees. There are two groves of giant sequoias, the Mariposa Grove and the Tuolumne Grove. We stopped at the Tuolumne Grove but only for a short while, as we got in the park late in the afternoon. We're going to be here all day tomorrow, so I'll write all about the park later. Right now I want to tell what happened today on the way here.

Mr. Glass's convention ended yesterday afternoon. Some of the people left right away, but we stayed on at the hotel overnight. About five o'clock, after everyone had said good-by, we walked to where Chinatown starts at Bush Street and Grant Avenue. The guide folder we picked up at the hotel said that San Francisco's Chinatown is the largest settlement of Chinese outside China. I can believe it, and all the Chinese run either curio shops or restaurants, most of them along Grant Avenue. We went in all of them, and my feet are still sore. I wonder why stores always have floors that hurt your feet. It's much easier walking on the sidewalk or street.

Some of the shops were very interesting—the first two or three blocks of them. All my life I've heard that the Chinese invented firecrackers and that they use them in all their celebrations. At the Chinese New Year they're supposed to shoot off tons of them. I guess they celebrated so much the last New Year's that they used up their supply, because they certainly didn't have any for sale. I can report definitely that it's useless to try to locate any in Chinatown. Everyone I asked gave me the same answer, "It's against the law." Mr. Glass said that if the underworld ever heard how scarce firecrackers were, it would probably quit smuggling diamonds and opium and turn to firecrackers.

Mr. Glass and I got tired of shopping after a while, but Mrs. Glass and Midge seemed to be nuclear-powered or something. There are eight blocks of shops, not counting the side streets, and they missed nothing. By the third block they had all the prices memorized and were comparing them from shop to shop. I bought a little bagful of dried sea horses. They are used as medicine by the Chinese. I don't know what I'll use them for, but they looked interesting. I also got some magic flowers. They are made of paper and are little tiny pellets. You drop one in water, and it expands into a big paper flower which floats.

Midge bought some Chinese jewelry, some embroidered pajamas, and some other junk. Then for some reason she started hunting for a gold nugget.

"Why would you expect to find a gold nugget in Chinatown?" I wanted to know. "And what do you want one for anyhow?"

"I want one so I can prove to my friends I've been to California," Midge said. "Everyone knows that California is where the big gold rush took place. There ought to be gold nuggets here. One is a must for the museum collection."

"What museum collection?" Mr. Glass asked.

"*Our* museum collection," Midge replied. "We're going to get something unusual or interesting from every important place we visit. Henry and I are going to open a travel museum when we get back."

"I see," said Mr. Glass thoughtfully. "I've got one suggestion."

"What's that?" Midge asked.

"Use a little judgment in picking these mementos," Mr. Glass said. "Remember, we have just an ordinary station wagon, not a trailer-truck, and there are four of us to travel all the way across the continent. We all have suitcases. Try to restrain yourselves and collect small items. Horses and elephants, for example, are out!"

Mr. Glass pretended to be joking, but I could tell he was serious about loading up the car. However, I don't know how horses and elephants got into the conversation.

"Gold nuggets are certainly small enough," Midge pointed out.

"You won't find any in Chinatown," I told her. "The Chinese didn't discover the gold in California."

I guess Midge didn't hear me, or if she did she certainly didn't pay much attention, because she kept right on looking for a gold nugget.

Midge could fall in a mud puddle and come up covered with daffodils. About two doors from where we were to eat dinner, a Chinese shopkeeper said, "Of course we have gold nuggets." He pulled out a big trayful. I'd never seen a gold nugget before, and I expected to see something more exciting. I had an idea they would be bright and shiny like a gold ring, but the shopkeeper explained that gold has to be smooth and polished before it shines. You could see that these nuggets were gold, but they were rough and dull. A hole had been bored in each one.

"What's that for?" Midge asked.

"You thread a chain through the hole and wear the nugget as a bracelet," the man explained.

Midge took about ten minutes pricing every nugget on the tray and finally picked one small one that cost fifteen dollars. The chain cost another two dollars. The bracelet certainly didn't look worth seventeen dollars to me, but Midge was as happy as though she had struck gold. It seems she had been planning on getting a gold nugget for months and had saved money for it, including some her grandmother had given her on her last birthday. Mrs. Glass said that she thought the bracelet was lovely, but Mr. Glass agreed with me. He didn't tell Midge that, but he said so to me.

"Some poor prospector probably trekked way up into

the mountains and went to a lot of trouble to find that nugget. He sold it and probably gave the money to some woman in his family, and she used it to buy a trinket that was made back in New Jersey. We take money from New Jersey and bring it out here to buy a gold nugget. That's commerce or trade, young man, and if you have enough transactions like that, everyone is supposed to become wealthy."

"I'd think they'd just be weighted down with bracelets," I said.

"You're probably right," Mr. Glass said. "But you're never going to be a famous economist if you keep poking holes in theories that way."

I don't know exactly what he meant, but it doesn't make much difference, because I'm going to be a naturalist and not an economist.

After Midge got her bracelet we went on to a restaurant for dinner. It was real Chinese food and very good. I had bird's-nest soup. I saw it on the menu and thought I'd try it. I didn't think it would actually be made from a bird's nest any more than Welsh rabbit is made from a rabbit. Then Midge asked the waiter when I was about halfway through if it actually was made with a bird's nest, and he said yes. In fact he told her all about how the birds' nests were gathered. I couldn't let Midge see how I felt, and I pretended I had known all along. In fact I even ate a few more spoonfuls although it wasn't easy. The rest of the dinner was delicious. We each ordered something different and then shared the dishes.

After dinner we walked back to the hotel. It was only nine o'clock when we arrived.

"We'll go right up and go to bed," Mr. Glass said. "Everyone do his best to go right to sleep, because we're going to get up early and be on our way. And by early I mean about five o'clock or so."

Mr. Glass paused at the desk to see if there were any messages. "There's nothing for you, sir," the clerk said. "I have a package and a message for a Miss Glass, though."

"That's me," Midge said promptly. "I wonder who is sending me something? Isn't it exciting, Henry?"

"Just a moment," the clerk said. He disappeared through a doorway and was gone several minutes. When he came back he had a cage in his hand. Inside the cage was a blue parakeet. The clerk put the cage on the counter and smiled at Midge. "For you, Miss Glass. There is a note in the envelope there." He pointed to an envelope that was fastened to one of the wires of the cage.

"It's Amos, I think," Midge said. "Doesn't it look like Amos, Henry?"

It was Amos. When I caught him earlier in the day one of his tail feathers had come out, and I could see the gap now.

"What is going on ?" Mr. Glass asked. "What is this parakeet doing here?"

43

"Maybe just visiting," Midge said. "The woman said he likes to go out. I suppose the note will tell me."

She untied the message, tore open the envelope, and read the note. "She's giving me Amos!" Midge said, squealing happily. "Isn't that wonderful?"

"She's doing no such thing!" Mr. Glass said firmly. "Let me see that letter. I'd like to know what this is all about."

Midge handed over the note and began talking to Amos. Midge gave me the note later, so I'll copy it exactly.

DEAR MISS GLASS:

You were so sweet and helpful this afternoon that I felt very guilty later when I realized that I had said only a brief "thank you." Your brother was very resourceful in rescuing poor Amos. I could tell from the way he was able to pick Amos off that light fixture that he knows how to handle little creatures. I know you both love animals and birds very much, so when I tried to think of a suitable reward, I thought of Amos himself. As I told you, I have fifteen birds so I won't miss him too much.

Amos is only a year old and is just learning to talk. I've taught him to say, "Good morning." I am afraid my mischievous nephew taught him to say, "You're too fat!" That is too close to the truth, which is one of the reasons I decided to give you Amos instead of one of the others. However, he'll probably forget this if you don't repeat it.

I remembered your name, of course, and recalled where you said you were staying. Please accept Amos with my thanks. I know you'll enjoy his company for many years to come.

Sincerely yours,
HANNAH HASKELL

"Of all the crazy ideas!" Mr. Glass exploded when he had finished reading the note. "We will just send Amos packing right back where he came from."

"There isn't any return address," Mrs. Glass said, looking over her husband's shoulder.

"Then we'll have to keep him," Midge said.

"We can't carry a blasted bird three thousand miles across the continent," Mr. Glass said.

"He's a good traveler," Midge said. "He likes to ride. We met him on a cable car. An automobile would be luxury after a cable car."

"For the bird, maybe, but not for us," Mr. Glass replied. "I can predict what would happen. The car would be full of birdseed in no time, not to mention bird droppings. How would you give the thing a drink?"

"When we stopped, I could give him a drink. Please, he won't take up much space. Besides, if we don't keep him what will happen to him? We can't abandon him."

"I can, without a qualm," Mr. Glass said sourly. "Or you can pack him off to an orphans' home. They have a home for everything else; there are probably homes for homeless parakeets too."

"He seems like a well-behaved bird," Mrs. Glass said, going up close to the cage. "How do you do, Amos."

Amos had been very quiet, sitting on his perch as though he were frightened or half asleep. He suddenly stretched his neck, let out two or three squawks, and then said, "Good morning, you're too fat!" His speech wasn't

45

too plain, but you could understand what he said.

"Hmm," said Mrs. Glass. "I'm not so sure you are so good."

Mr. Glass had been looking like a thundercloud, but now he grinned. He's a tall, stringy man with a bald head. Mrs. Glass is rather short and, while she isn't fat, she is rather well padded. She had put on some more padding since I saw her last summer. Several times in the short while I've been with them she has complained about the meals being too large, so I guess she is watching her weight.

Midge was watching both her parents, and she decided this was her opportunity. "We can't do anything tonight. Let's keep him a few days, and if he's too much trouble in the car, we can always give him away."

Mr. Glass shrugged his shoulders. "If we do, he's your responsibility entirely. And don't complain if something happens to him, as I predict it will if he doesn't keep his mouth shut."

"I suppose that remark was intended for me, Ernie," Mrs. Glass said. "You know perfectly well I'm not sensitive about that subject, particularly if the comments come from a parakeet. I suppose we'll have to find some birdseed first thing tomorrow."

"The lady left a package of birdseed," the desk clerk said. "I'm sorry, I almost forgot that."

Midge carried the parakeet as we all went up to bed. It seemed to me that I had just gone to sleep when the telephone rang and the operator said, "It's quarter after five, sir." I looked outside, and it seemed more like quarter after three. Even after we all assembled in the lobby it was so dark you could hardly see the street lights through the fog.

The dining room in the hotel wasn't open, it was so early. We started out without any breakfast and were miles outside Oakland by seven-thirty, when we stopped to eat. By noon we were well into the foothills and not many miles from Yosemite. Mrs. Glass had bought some meat, bread, and other groceries in a town called Manteca. We had put the food and some soft drinks in a little ice chest in the back of the station wagon. It was a good thing, too, because there wasn't any place to buy anything for miles and miles outside Yosemite National Park. The country kept getting wilder and the road more twisty and turny as we headed up into the mountains. The scenery kept improving, too, and finally we pulled off the road at a beautiful spot with pine trees all around and a rushing stream. Mr. Glass looked at the map and said the stream might be the Tuolumne River or one of its branches.

"Look at all this beautiful empty country," he said, stretching his arms. "This is officially my first day of vacation, and I'm going to celebrate by taking a nap right out here in the wide open spaces. After listening for five solid days to chemists lecturing for at least eight hours a day and then yammering half the night, nothing could sound so beautiful to me as all this quiet. And think of it, not another human being in sight as far as we can see!"

47

There was a carrier on top of the station wagon in addition to a rear end full of gear. Mr. Glass had come prepared for everything. He rooted around in the car and from somewhere produced a bright red hammock. He picked two pine trees and stretched his hammock. Then, as soon as we had had lunch, he stretched out in the hammock. Mrs. Glass had bought a cherry pie, and before Midge and I had finished the last, we could hear him snoring.

Mrs. Glass got out a blanket and, using it for a cushion, leaned back against a tree and began reading. "There are two fishing rods in there somewhere," she said. "Why don't you two try your luck."

48

I got out one of the rods, but Midge wasn't interested. She looked at the aluminum pie plate that had held the cherry pie and said, "I know, I'll go pan for gold."

"I guess we aren't too far from gold country," Mrs. Glass said, looking up from her book. "And as a bit of miscellaneous information, the gold rush of 1848 was started by James Marshall who came from near where we live in New Jersey."

"Where?" Midge asked.

"He was born in Hunterdon County," Mrs. Glass replied. "Marshall's Corner near Hopewell was named after the Marshall family."

"If he could discover gold, I can too," Midge said, grabbing the aluminum pan. "Let's go."

We walked over to the stream. Midge took off her shoes and waded in, and I started casting a short distance downstream from her. The water was beautiful and clear, and I couldn't see any fish or gold, but I tried and so did she. After about ten minutes of poking around in the stream and examining several pans of gravel, she called to me.

"I haven't discovered any gold yet," she said. "Maybe I'm not doing it right. How are you supposed to pan gold anyhow? And why use a pan in the first place?"

"I've never panned gold but I read about it someplace," I told her. "You are supposed to fill the pan with fine gravel. Then you swirl it around and wash the gravel out over the edge. The gold sinks to the bottom and when most of the gravel is gone, there it'll be."

"Sounds simple," Midge said. "I ought to be able to do it."

I had worked downstream a short distance, and just below me was a nice shallow spot with pebbles and sand on the bottom. Midge came down to try her luck there. By this time we were several hundred yards from where Mr. Glass was snoring in the hammock.

Midge waded out into the stream and began rotating the panful of gravel like a real gold prospector. On the second panful she looked up and said in a very excited voice, "Hank! Gold! I've really found some!"

I didn't believe her, but I put down my fishing pole and waded out to where she was standing.

"Look!" she said. "A gold nugget!"

I looked, and there was a nugget of gold all right. I started to get excited, and then I picked up the nugget and saw that it had a hole in it.

"Odd the way water drilled such a neat hole through it," I said. "Why don't you put a gold chain through it and use it as a bracelet?"

"Phooey!" Midge said. "I should have covered up the hole."

She was chewing gum so she took a tiny piece, plugged the hole at both ends, and smeared the gum with a little dirt.

"It looks genuine now," she said. "If I'd done that in the first place I think I'd have caught you. I'll do it over again and you pretend to be surprised."

"All right," I said. "If I'm not busy catching a fish."

She pretended to pan gold for a minute or two and then yelled excitedly. "Hank! I've done it. I've found gold. Come look."

"All right," I said. "I don't believe it but I'll look."

She handed over the pan, pointing at the nugget. "See, isn't that a gold nugget?"

"It looks like gold," I said, going along with her game. "Maybe you've struck it rich, pardner."

"Let me see it," a strange voice said, causing us both to jump with surprise.

We turned around, and standing a yard or two upstream

was a heavy-set man in a khaki shirt and trousers, a safety helmet, and engineer's boots. He had a round red face which was covered with perspiration. He looked like a man from a road construction outfit, which, it turned out later, was exactly what he was.

Both Midge and I felt foolish and embarrassed. To begin with we hadn't thought anyone was around for miles except for the occasional car that buzzed by on the highway. Secondly, we wouldn't have been playing such a silly game out loud if we'd thought anyone might be listening. Neither of us knew exactly what to do—whether to tell the man we were kidding or just to keep quiet. Before we could decide, the man waded out several steps and held out his hand. Midge looked at me, raised her eyebrows, and handed him the pan without a word.

It didn't take the man five seconds to locate the nugget. He picked it up from the gravel between a blunt forefinger and thumb and held it at eye level.

"Well I'll be! You have found a nugget, sis, and a nice one! This is amazing. I would have bet that every inch of this stream had been prospected seventy-five years ago."

He was holding the nugget in his right hand, almost at arm's length, while he kept fumbling in his shirt pocket with his left hand. I've seen my father do that hundreds of times, and I knew what the trouble was. He was farsighted and had to use glasses to see anything close. Several times when Dad mislaid his glasses I've seen him back off a good yard from a telephone book before he could read a number.

"Wish I had my glasses," the man finally mumbled, "but even without 'em I can tell that it's real gold. It looks a bit polished, which may mean that it has tumbled downstream for quite a distance." He paused and looked thoughtfully at the rushing stream. He seemed to be talking out loud to himself and to have forgotten that we were there. "I suppose the only thing to do would be to start here someplace and to work slowly upstream for several miles. Wonder what I've got in the truck."

He turned back toward the edge of the stream. Midge started to get alarmed.

"Could I have my nugget, please?" she asked.

"Sorry, I didn't mean to walk off with it," the man said with a smile. He took a long last look at it and handed it back to Midge. Then he hurried off through the brush.

Midge began to giggle. "He believed us, Hank! We may not find a gold mine, but we'll make a fortune on the stage. That was superb acting, Mr. Reed."

"I wasn't acting after he appeared," I said. "Let's see where he goes."

We climbed out on the bank and walked around a clump of bushes. Parked beside the road was a pickup truck and behind it a dump truck. Two or three men were seated on the ground nearby. They had apparently stopped for lunch. The man we had talked to was hurrying toward them.

They stood together in a group for a few minutes, and then two of them began rummaging around in a tool chest in the back of the truck. They took out something that looked like a bunch of tin cans, and then one man jumped in the cab and roared off down the road.

"He's gone back after something they can use to pan gold," I said. "In the meantime, the others are going to try with those tin cans."

"Goody, goody, I've started a gold rush!" Midge said, jumping up and down. "Wait until I tell the kids at school about this."

"Go get your camera," I suggested. "I'll get back in the stream and pretend I'm looking for more gold. It would look suspicious if we rushed off after making a find."

I picked up the pan and went back into the stream. I filled it with gravel and began panning. As long as I was going through the motions I decided to do it right. After all, I might really find something.

In a few minutes I was joined by the red-faced man and a tall, leathery-faced companion. They both waded out into the stream and looked around.

"Well, it could be," the tall man said. "It doesn't look too likely, but then gold is found in some unlikely places. And as you say, maybe it has been carried downstream. We ought to find some dust in that case."

"How are you coming, son? Find anything else?" the red-faced man asked.

"No nuggets," I said truthfully. "Or at least none that I noticed."

"How about dust?"

"I'm not sure what dust looks like," I told him.

"Like little pieces of sand, only bright and shiny as you would expect gold to be."

I shook my head. "No. But I haven't been looking too closely. I want to find a nugget like Midge's."

"Would you mind showing that to my friend Jim?" the red-faced man asked.

"She took it back up to the car," I hedged. "After you told her it was really gold, she decided she'd better put it away."

Midge arrived at the same time as two other men. They seemed to know the first two and gave them pans. All four men started panning industriously. Two moved a short distance upstream.

"Jed overheard me so I suppose it will be all over," one of the newcomers remarked.

Midge took one picture of all four men and me in the stream and then had to change her film. While she was doing that three or four others arrived. Then apparently some tourists stopped, intending to eat lunch, but they got the gold fever too. They must have known something about panning gold, because they took one look at the stream and inside of a minute they were out in it too. How the news spread so fast way out there in the wilderness, I'll never know. I suppose people driving by saw all the parked cars and became curious. Each new parked car made it worse. At first they asked Midge and me what it was all about, because we were standing on the stream bank watching.

"Someone found a gold nugget," I said, which was somewhat near the truth.

Midge made no effort to stay within miles of the facts. She had a wonderful time stirring up everyone. "I think it's an important gold strike," she told one man in red-checked shorts and a bright blue sport shirt. "That one man way upstream is an old prospector, and he says this is a rich find."

It wasn't long before Midge and I weren't needed. Some of the later arrivals began talking, telling about huge nuggets that had been found by the dozen. Midge was running

all over taking pictures. The bigger the crowd got the more fun she had.

"Oh, oh, I think I heard Pop calling," she said suddenly.

"I think it'd be just as well if we got out of here anyhow," I said.

"I've got one more exposure. Let me get one last shot of the famous Glass Gold Diggings and we'll leave."

When we got back to where the station wagon was parked we found that Mr. Glass had packed his hammock, and everything was loaded and ready to go.

"Who'd believe it?" Mr. Glass said grumpily. "I pick out

the loneliest spot I've seen in months. I stretch my hammock and go to sleep with not a soul within miles. Half an hour later the place looks like a parking lot outside a football stadium on a game day. People are milling all over and shouting to each other to hurry. The place is a madhouse. What in the world happened, anyhow? Was someone hurt or did some fool get eaten by a grizzly bear?"

"There's a gold rush," Midge said. "A real genuine, honest-to-goodness, cross-my-heart gold rush."

"Gold rush my eye!"

"That's really it, isn't it, Hank?"

"That's what the excitement is about," I agreed. "Everybody is down at the stream panning for gold."

"Hmm," said Mr. Glass. "I don't know too much about gold prospecting, but I wouldn't pick this area as likely. Still, if somebody has made a find it might be worth investigating. It would be fun to find a few flakes of gold so I could say I'd actually found gold."

"I don't think I'd waste the time, Mr. Glass," I said.

We were all in the car except Mr. Glass. He was standing outside the driver's seat with his head inside, looking back at Midge and me. Just then Amos woke up and said, "Good morning. You're too fat. You're too fat." Then he gave four or five screeches that sounded like an idiot laughing.

Mr. Glass waited until the parakeet quieted down, took a deep breath, and asked, "Just why are you advising me not to waste my time?"

"I think I found more gold than anybody," Midge said

58

in a small voice. "All I did was to look at my gold nugget, and suddenly it was like a forest fire."

"I see," Mr. Glass said. Without another word he got into the car and started toward Yosemite.

"We didn't really do a thing," Midge said. "I was just pretending to find a nugget, and this man came up and insisted on examining it. He took over from there."

"That's what Henry's Uncle Al warned me would happen," Mr. Glass said. "He said you two would do something perfectly innocent and blameless and then suddenly strange things would happen as a result. Where are we staying tonight, Hazel?"

"At the Big Trees Lodge," Mrs. Glass said. "That's right in the Mariposa Grove of giant sequoias."

"I don't know that it's safe," Mr. Glass said. "Midge, both you and Henry turn in your pocketknives before you go to bed. I don't want one of those big redwoods falling on us."

Naturally he was kidding, because anyone knows you couldn't cut a big redwood tree down with a pocketknife in a year. He didn't seem to be joking, though. I suppose scientists like Mr. Glass get pretty tired out and really need their vacation. I think this vacation will do a lot for him.

Monday, June 21st—Big Trees Lodge,
Yosemite National Park, California

Tonight will be our third night in Yosemite National Park. We are staying at some very nice cabins right in the middle of the Mariposa Grove of giant sequoia trees. It is wonderful stepping out of your cabin in the morning and looking up at those enormous trees. Midge says they give her an inferiority complex, but I don't think she really means it. They do make a person seem tiny, though. The Grizzly Giant is thirty-five feet in diameter and over two hundred feet tall. Wawona, which is a little way up the road, is about two hundred and thirty-four feet high and has a tunnel you can drive through. I wish a kid I knew in Naples named Bucky O'Reilly was here. He was always bragging that he could climb any tree. I'd tell him to skin up one of these.

We have had a wonderful time here. We've taken two hikes; we spent one morning on a horseback trip; and we went up to see the waterfalls and the view from Glacier Point. The guide said yesterday that Upper Yosemite Falls is nine times as high as Niagara Falls. So much water comes over it that you can feel the ground shake a quarter of a mile away. We're here at just the right time because by the middle of July most of the snow in the mountains has melted, and the falls practically disappear.

The mountains look very much like the Alps, only they're wilder-looking. The trees are much prettier than in the Alps, and there is much more wildlife. I guess the only thing that Switzerland has that Yosemite hasn't is Swiss chocolate.

The water in the stream is beautiful and clear, and it's deep enough in a number of places to go swimming. Midge and I tried it and almost froze to death. There is good fishing, though, and I would just as soon fish as swim. You can lie on a rock and look down into the clear water and watch the fish, which is more fun than catching them.

I wish we could stay longer. When I'm through school and am a naturalist, I'm going to come back for a really long visit. These three days have been perfect except for a little pest who is staying in the next cabin with her grandparents. Her name is Cindy Mayhew. I suppose she's ten or eleven. My grandparents never let me boss them around the way she does hers. The grandfather is lame and uses a cane. Neither he nor the grandmother can climb mountain trails and things like that. We felt sorry for Cindy at first, and we took her on one hike and a horseback trip. She complained the whole time and tried to boss everyone. The way she kept yelling "Henreeeee!" drove me crazy. She was scared of everything. She's from Chicago, and I can understand that they don't have many wild animals running around in a big city, but there must be bugs. Cindy screeched every time a bug touched her.

This girl wears her hair loose like a mane, which is probably a good style for her since she has a long enough face and nose for a horse. She may not know anything about wildlife or nature, but she thinks she knows everything else. And after this trip she'll be the expert on Yosemite in the Chicago area. Last night we went to a campfire lecture by one of the rangers. Cindy was there, and she came over to sit beside Midge and me.

The lecture was about the redwoods and how many thousands of years it takes for one to grow to full size. There are very few left as most of them have been cut down by lumber companies and sawed up into boards. I thought the talk was very interesting, and at least Cindy kept quiet while the ranger was talking. The minute he stopped, though, she began. She went on and on about how awful it was to destroy a beautiful thing like a redwood tree until I was hoping one would fall on her. Midge was tired of listening to her, too, but there wasn't much we could do unless we wanted to leave and miss the second half of the talk.

"I think they're big ungainly trees," Midge said, just to be different. "They should be made into toothpicks. Just think of all the poor people in the world who haven't any toothpicks, and these trees would supply them."

Just at that minute I felt something crawling on my arm. I looked, and it was a small bug similar to a ladybug only much lighter in color. I was examining it when Cindy spotted it.

"Ugh, how can you stand to hold a horrible bug like that?"

There wasn't anything horrible about the bug at all. It was a nice, polite bug. I like bugs if they don't bite or sting, and the hundreds of different kinds are just as interesting as birds and a lot easier to catch.

"This little bug could climb to the top of that redwood if it wanted to. That's more than you or I can do." I gave Midge a poke with my elbow. "Do you know what kind of bug this is?" I asked Cindy.

"No."

"It's a termite," I said. "A very special kind of termite —a real Siberian termite."

"What's a Siberian termite?" Cindy asked.

"Do you know what an ordinary termite is?"

She didn't, so I told her a little bit about termites, all of which was true.

"Termites can eat the sills and rafters in your house until it falls down," Midge said in a very serious voice. "And Siberian termites are ten times as bad. No one but a few etymologists and Henry . . ."

"Entomologists," I said.

"Just a few scientists know about Siberian termites and how destructive they are," Midge said.

I had a small plastic box in my pocket that I used to hold

fishhooks. I dumped the fishhooks into my shirt pocket while Cindy wasn't looking and popped the bug into the box. As I did I spotted a second bug of the same kind on the collar of the man ahead of me. I pretended to stretch and picked it up in the process. I slipped it into the box with the other bug.

"I have a pair," I said, holding up the box. "I let one out at a time now and then for a little exercise."

"What do you feed them?" Cindy asked.

"Redwood. I give them a big splinter every morning. They love it."

"If he let them out they would eat up a whole tree," Midge said solemnly.

"Two little bugs couldn't eat a great big tree in a million years," Cindy said. She showed some common sense now and then.

"No, but a million Siberian termites could," Midge said. "You've heard how flies multiply. They aren't in it with these termites. In a few months there would be millions if Henry let those two loose. And in nothing flat they'd chew up all the big trees and be starting on the small ones. Then New Jersey would have trees just as big as California's."

"You wouldn't do a thing like that, would you?" Cindy asked.

"I might," I said, looking as threatening as possible.

"The giant sequoia is one of the noblest creations of nature," Cindy said. "It would be awful to let bugs eat them."

If the bugs had really been Siberian termites that loved

redwood, I would have been tempted to let them out. If Cindy had said that line about the giant sequoias being one of nature's noblest creations once, she had said it fifty times. Midge and I had read the same little folder which was in every cabin.

The second half of the lecture started, so I didn't think anything more about the Siberian termites until we were on our way back to the cabin. Then one of the fishhooks stuck me, so I let the bugs go and put my fishhooks back in the plastic box.

The next morning on our way to breakfast we met Cindy. She looked worried. I guess she had been awake half the night thinking about those bugs, because the first thing she asked about was the termites.

"Could I see them again?" she asked.

"They're home eating a big piece of redwood," Midge said promptly. "We'll show them to you when we get back."

Cindy finished breakfast before we did and left, saying she would see us at the cabin.

"We'll either have to duck her or tell her it was all a joke," I told Midge. "I let the bugs go."

"Maybe we can catch a couple more," Midge said. "We've got too good a plot to give up now."

We looked around for bugs on the way back, but I couldn't find a one like those of the night before. I turned over a rotten piece of wood and several black bugs scurried out, but they were about twice the size of the ones last night.

66

"Catch them," Midge said. "They'll do."

"Don't be ridiculous," I said. "Even Cindy will know they're not the same bugs. Look how much bigger they are, and they aren't the same shape."

Midge never lets little things like facts bother her when she decides upon something. She argued that if a worm or a grub in a cocoon can change overnight into a butterfly, there's no reason why a small reddish bug can't change into a bigger black one. Of course that argument doesn't make sense, because bugs don't change that way even if butterflies do. Anyhow, to keep her happy I caught two black bugs and carried them back to the cabin in my handkerchief. I put them in the little plastic box and gave them to Midge.

"You explain how they got so big," I said.

"Why, everybody that knows anything about Siberian termites knows they thrive on a diet of redwood," she said.

Mr. Glass and I decided to go fishing. Mrs. Glass and Midge were going to visit the museum when it opened at ten o'clock. Before any of us could get started anywhere, Cindy appeared.

"Could I see the termites?" she asked.

Midge had brought Amos out to clean his cage and to give him a little sunshine. She set the cage down on the ground and went back in for the bugs.

"They certainly do grow on redwood," Midge said, handing the box to Cindy. "Overnight they've developed into

67

the next stage. Now they'll lay thousands of eggs, and there'll be swarms of them."

"Margaret, look what I found," Mrs. Glass called.

She was standing on the opposite side of the road, a short distance back in the trees. In her hand was a pine cone almost as big as her head. Midge ran over to look, and I kept on trying to undo a tangle in my fish line. No one paid any attention to Cindy. Suddenly I heard Midge shout. "Where's Amos?"

Amos was gone. His cage was still where Midge had left it but there wasn't a feather of Amos left anywhere. I walked over to take a closer look. The door of the cage was open and on the floor was my plastic fishhook box. It was open, and the bugs were gone. It was a clean sweep.

"Where's Cindy?" Midge asked, after she had examined everything. "She had that box a minute ago."

We looked around, but Cindy had disappeared as completely as the parakeet and the termites.

"Maybe a mountain lion got the lot of them," I suggested.

At that moment Midge spotted Cindy peeking out from behind one of the cabins. "Cindy, you come here and tell me what happened, or I'll come after you!" Midge shouted.

Cindy started slowly toward us, looking like a frightened chipmunk.

"They're loose," she said finally in a small, scared voice. "I tried to stop them but they got away. It was all Amos' fault."

"What was?" Midge asked. "And where is Amos?"

"He flew away. I didn't want the termites to eat all the redwoods. I didn't know how to kill them so I opened the box and put it inside the cage. But Amos wouldn't eat them; he just flew away!" She ended with a wail like a sick puppy.

"Where?" Midge demanded.

"They crawled off through the grass!"

"Oh, forget the bugs!" Midge said. "What became of Amos?"

"I don't know! Now all the trees will be eaten!"

"Quit blubbering, and help us find Amos," I said. Sobbing women always make me lose my temper.

We hunted for the next fifteen minutes, but Amos had apparently taken off for the top of the redwoods, and I figured nothing but a helicopter would have much chance of locating him. Mr. Glass came out with his fishing gear and naturally wanted to know what all the fuss was about.

"Serves you right," he said, after Midge had explained. "You shouldn't have tried to hoodwink the poor little girl."

"Poor little girl, my eye!" Midge said. "She's a pest. How are we going to find Amos?"

"Probably we never will," Mr. Glass said happily. "You should have taught him our address, and then he could have asked directions. A month or two of steady flying would put him on our back porch."

"I don't think it would take that long," I said. "Pigeons will fly three hundred miles a day."

"Well, let's hope Amos is really a pigeon and flies back to his original home," Mr. Glass said.

It was easy to see that Mr. Glass wasn't going to help much, and I couldn't think of anything to do, so we went fishing. We had a good time, wading up and down in the stream, but we didn't catch many fish. We got back to the cabin about noon. There was Midge sitting on the little front step of the cabin, her chin in her hands, looking very blue.

"I've called until I'm hoarse," she said. "Not even a peep from him."

A park ranger drove by, and I flagged him. "She's lost her parakeet," I explained. "Do you know how to get a parakeet back?"

The ranger was very nice. "Let me think," he said, rubbing his chin. "I read one time about some method of attracting a bird back to his cage if he gets away outdoors."

"They're afraid of being out if they've spent their life in a cage," I said. "That's home to them."

"I know," the ranger said. "You spread a sheet and put the cage in the middle of it. That lets the bird spot his cage easier. You haven't got another bird, have you? A decoy might help."

"The only place I know where there are any others is San Francisco," Midge said gloomily. "I doubt if Dad would drive me back. He's glad Amos got away."

"If a dead bird would be of any help I could get you a frozen scrub jay," the ranger said with a grin.

"A frozen jay?" I asked suspiciously.

"I picked one up along the road the other day. I suppose a car hit it. When we find a bird in good shape we take it to headquarters and put it in the freezer in case anyone wants it for mounting. No one wants this one, so he'll be thrown out. If a wooden duck will attract ducks, why won't a frozen jay attract a parakeet?"

I had my doubts about the scheme, but I rode down to headquarters with him and got the jay. By the time we got back, Midge had spread the sheet and had put the cage in the center of it. With the help of a paper clip and a rubber band I managed to get the jay to sit on Amos' perch. He looked very lifelike—just a little stiff. Then everybody went to lunch. By the time lunch was over, the jay had thawed enough that his head was beginning to slump. We were debating whether or not we should take him out when Cindy appeared.

"Did Amos come back?" she asked.

"You can see," Midge said. She was still annoyed at Cindy.

"He looks much bigger and different."

"That's what happens when a parakeet gets out and eats the wrong kind of feed," Midge said, beginning to take a little more interest in life. "He swells up and dies."

It was perfect timing. She had scarcely finished when the "parakeet" toppled forward and fell off the perch.

"Well, that's it," Midge said, with a catch in her voice.

"There's nothing left to do but have the funeral and bury him."

We found a piece of board for a shovel and took the dead jay into the woods and buried it. The funeral was a big success. I acted as minister. Cindy cried, which is what she deserved. When we got back to the cabin the bird cage and the sheet had disappeared. We went inside, and there was Amos in his cage on the bureau.

"I looked out and there he was hopping around on the sheet," Mrs. Glass said. "I waited a few minutes, and he hopped inside. I couldn't find either of you, so I went up quietly and closed the door."

Cindy hadn't come inside with us, and as far as I know, she still thinks we buried Amos. We didn't see her again. Mrs. Glass said later she thought we were mean not to leave a note telling Cindy the truth. I'm not so certain. I'd like to listen in when she gets back to Chicago and starts telling her friends about the Wild West. The cowboys will have to take second place to my Siberian termites.

Tuesday, June 22nd—Los Angeles, California

Well, here we are in Los Angeles. Los Angeles is supposed to cover more territory than any other city in the United States, according to an article I read. You'd think in all that area someone would sell firecrackers, but no one does. I've seen a few signs that said "Fireworks," but when I investigated all they had was a few sparklers, some caps, and some sick-looking Roman candles.

We haven't made much progress driving across the country. We went east from San Francisco to Yosemite, but now we're back again, practically beside the ocean. Mr.

Glass has a business appointment here, and then we are going across the United States by the southern route.

We arrived at our hotel late this afternoon. We made very good time from Yosemite in spite of all the wind resistance. I think maybe Mr. Glass was wrong about how much the wind would slow us down. We moved right along at fifty to sixty miles an hour in spite of the big bag of pine cones.

At breakfast this morning Midge said that she wanted to pick up some pine cones to take home for her travel museum. Mr. Glass didn't pay too much attention.

"See that you get a bag to put them in," he said. "I don't want them kicking around all over the car."

Midge and I finished eating before Mr. and Mrs. Glass, and we hurried back to get the pine cones. On our way to the cabins we passed some trash cans that had been set out for collection and on top of one was a big burlap bag. It wasn't just an ordinary feed bag but one of those great big ones that they use for dried citrus pulp.

"That's just what we need," Midge said. "The perfect size."

"For what?" I asked. "An elephant?"

"Pine cones," Midge said.

"Your father wants to get going," I told her. "We won't have time to gather up all the pine cones in the park."

"If we can find those big ones, we won't be five minutes."

She was right. A short distance from the cabin we found a place littered with enormous cones. They weren't from the giant sequoias but from other huge pines. We gathered a few of each variety we could find, but we filled most of the bag with the big ones. In a few minutes it was full, and together we carried it back to the station wagon. The station wagon has a chrome rail around the top and a luggage carrier near the rear. We hoisted the bag up and put it in front of the luggage carrier. I found some heavy cord and tied the front corners to the chrome rail and the rear corners to the luggage carrier.

"Perfect," Midge said when I finished. "Dad can't object to the pine cones kicking around the car when they're not even inside."

Mr. Glass did object, though. I'd done a neat job, but he didn't appreciate it. He took one look at the car when he got back and let out a bellow. "What is that monstrosity?"

"Pine cones," Midge said. "A bagful of pine cones."

"What did you do? Strip the western slope of the Sierra Nevadas of all the pine cones?"

"There aren't many," Midge said. "They're this big." She held up her hands to show him how big.

"Oh, you found some more of those?" Mrs. Glass asked. "I saw only one good one yesterday. If you gilded them, they'd make lovely Christmas decorations for the house."

"We're six months from Christmas and three thousand miles from the house," Mr. Glass said. "Do you expect to drive across the continent looking like a troupe of bankrupt hobos with our belongings tied to the top of the car in a burlap bag?"

"People won't think we're bankrupt with a nice-looking car like ours," Mrs. Glass said. "We can get something in Los Angeles that looks a little neater than that burlap bag."

"I've got a suggestion," Mr. Glass said. "Why don't we let the parakeet go, since he seems to like it here? Then we can fill his cage with pine cones, throw the others away, and do the same with the burlap bag."

My father is in the diplomatic service, and he says that there are many times when the most diplomatic thing one can say is nothing. I figured this was one of them. I kept very quiet. Finally Mr. Glass let Midge keep the bag of pine cones, but he grumbled all the way to Los Angeles. Every time anyone passed us he said it was because of the wind resistance of that bag on top of the car. Also, each time we passed under a bridge or overpass, he read the clearance.

"Thirteen feet clearance," he would say. "I doubt if we'll get through with that big bump on top."

I don't think he is a very good judge of distance, though, because we got under all the bridges easily. Mr. Glass kept complaining about having to drive up to the hotel with that bag on top of the car, but the people there didn't even glance at us. My father says that Los Angeles is full of lunatics, so I guess they thought we were normal.

Los Angeles isn't nearly as interesting a city as San Francisco. It's sprawled all over. I guess the reason it's so scattered is that it is so full of expressways and traffic circles and approaches to the superhighways that there isn't any room for buildings. Mr. Glass said that he heard a man got lost in the middle of Los Angeles in one of their super-highway tangles. The traffic was moving so fast he couldn't stop, and the smog was so thick he couldn't see the signs, so he starved to death before he could find his way to civilization. I think that is just a story, though, because you would run out of gas before you would starve to death.

Right across from the hotel is a parklike area called Pershing Square. We walked around it just as it was getting dark. I think the odd characters that my father mentioned must have all gathered at one time in the square. Every few feet someone was making a speech. Half of them had only one or two listeners, and even they weren't paying much attention.

"Listen to them," Mrs. Glass said. "And you were afraid of attracting attention because of a burlap bag full of pine cones."

"Some one of these fanatics ought to be able to foresee the future," Mr. Glass said. "I'd like to get a few prophecies about this trip we have ahead of us. I want to know where I'm going to sit while I drive by the time we hit Kansas. At the rate we're going it's obvious there won't be room inside the car."

Wednesday, June 23rd—Los Angeles

Today has been quiet. There's not much to see in Los Angeles and not much for a visitor to do. I suppose it's a nice place to live, because an awful lot of people live here, and there must be a reason. There isn't much I can say in my travel book about it, though, except that Los Angeles is the reason someone invented air conditioning.

I'm writing this in the hotel lobby while we wait for Mr. Glass, who is seeing someone on business. It's only three o'clock but as soon as he gets back we're driving out to Disneyland. We're going to spend a while there and then leave about eleven or twelve o'clock and drive to Las Vegas, Nevada. Mr. Glass says the only time to drive across the desert is at night.

I'm looking forward to Disneyland—especially since today has been so quiet. In fact it would have been really dull except for the monkey we saw.

Mr. Glass went out on business this morning and agreed to meet the rest of us at Olvera Street at twelve-thirty. Mrs. Glass drove us around in the car to show us a little bit of Los Angeles, and then we parked near one end of Olvera Street about eleven. Olvera Street is one of the oldest streets in Los Angeles and is supposed to look the way the Mexican streets did years ago. It's filled with booths that sell Mexican handicrafts, paintings, and everything except firecrackers. There are restaurants and artists' booths and a number of interesting shops. Of course the shops were a lot more interesting to Mrs. Glass and to Midge than to me. After I'd been in three or four, my feet began to get tired.

Olvera Street is only about two blocks long, and you aren't allowed to drive through but have to walk. In fact there are so many curio stands in the middle of the street that you couldn't possibly drive through. I bought a Mexican billfold at one shop, and after that I lost interest. I tagged along after Mrs. Glass and Midge. They went in and out of every shop and managed to make those two blocks last forever. What puzzles me most about women shoppers is that they will spend ten minutes examining something they don't have any idea of buying.

I was getting tired of Olvera Street when I saw a monkey. It came walking along all by itself, dressed up with a little cap and suit like an organ-grinder's monkey, but there was no organ or organ-grinder. The visitors all looked, but none of the shopkeepers paid any attention. I guess they knew he wasn't a likely customer.

"A loose monkey just went by," I told a woman in one of the stands.

"That's Diego," she said. "He won't bother anything. He's looking for someone to give him some peanuts."

"Doesn't he belong to anyone?"

"Old Charlie. He's probably eating lunch somewhere. Diego won't leave Olvera Street. He often wanders around by himself."

I bought a bag of peanuts and offered several to Diego. He took them, bowed politely, and then stared at me while he ate them. I was feeding him more, one at a time, and getting along fine when Midge and her mother came out of the shop where they had been looking around.

"Who's your friend?" Midge asked.

"Diego. Diego, this is Mrs. Glass and Miss Glass."

I slipped him another peanut without Midge seeing me, and he bowed. Midge was delighted, and even Mrs. Glass was impressed.

"Why, he's very polite," Mrs. Glass said. "In fact considerably more polite than some children I've known."

Midge bought some candy-covered popcorn for Diego. Either he liked us, or he saw that we were easy marks for peanuts and popcorn. As we started down the street, he came along, chattering and jumping around us in a circle. Mrs. Glass normally isn't much interested in animals, but Diego made quite an impression. She even borrowed some peanuts from me and fed him. Something about Mrs. Glass fascinated Diego, because he kept looking up at her and dancing in front of her, paying much, much more attention to her than to Midge or me.

"Wait until I tell Dad this," Midge whispered. "When he

hears Mom made a terrific hit with a monkey, he'll be jealous."

We came to a stand in the middle of the street that sold baskets, and Mrs. Glass stopped to look at several of them. Suddenly Diego leaped up on the counter and reached out his paw. Mrs. Glass was bending over something on the counter, and Diego grabbed one of her earrings and yanked. Mrs. Glass gave a yelp, half from surprise and half because it hurt. Diego jumped down from the counter and leaped up and down on the pavement, chattering and waving his arms.

"Give that back at once!" Mrs. Glass said.

Diego jumped up and down like a rubber monkey, ran around in circles, leaped up on the counter, swung from a rack over the counter, and then leaped down again, all the time chattering like a lunatic. He put on quite a show, and in nothing flat we had a crowd around us. About the only thing he didn't do was drop the earring. He was chattering angrily, and the crowd began to look at Mrs. Glass as though she were guilty of beating him or something equally mean.

"He has my earring," Mrs. Glass explained to no one in particular. "And I must have it back."

"What did you give it to him for?" a man asked.

"I didn't!" Mrs. Glass explained, getting annoyed. "The little beast stole it."

She tried to coax Diego to come close, but he would have

81

nothing to do with her. He scampered up on top of an awning and sat there making faces and probably swearing at her in monkey language.

"Henry, you're good with animals," she said. "See if you can coax him down. That earring isn't particularly valuable, but it means a lot to me."

I knew I couldn't do anything with all the people around, but in a minute or two they began to drift away since there was no more excitement. I told Midge and her mother to go on up the street while I tried to coax Diego down. After a few minutes he stopped chattering, and finally he jumped down from the awning. I offered him a peanut, which he ate with his left hand, this time without bowing. On the third peanut, I managed to take hold of his left arm. I did it very gently, and he didn't object. Then I tried to open his right hand. He went into a screaming, chattering rage and almost pulled away from me. He had that fist so tightly closed that I could see prying it open would be difficult. It was amazing how much strength he had in those little fingers.

As soon as I had caught Diego, Mrs. Glass came back.

"I've got him but I can't get the earring," I explained. "And I don't know how long I'll be able to hold him if he starts to scratch or bite."

"Oh dear, I suppose I'll have to locate his owner," Mrs. Glass said. "Can you hold him awhile? I'm afraid if we let him go he's liable to drop the earring or hide it some place."

"Why doesn't Henry take him to the car, and then he won't have to hold him? He can stay in the car with him while we go hunt for the organ-grinder."

We decided that was the best course of action. Mrs. Glass gave me the keys, and I took Diego to the car. I got in with him and rolled down the windows an inch or so for air. Then I let him go. We were in the second seat, and he promptly jumped into the front and began honking the horn and playing with the steering wheel. I thought he might get so interested he would drop the earring, so I let him honk. I slid way down so that he would think he was alone and would relax.

A minute or two later a police patrol car pulled up along-side. I suppose the noise of the horn attracted them.

"Get a load of this, Jim," a voice said. "Do you suppose he's got a license?"

"Could be," the other patrolman said. "That's a Jersey tag, isn't it? I've heard about Jersey drivers all my life."

"Hey, that was Erdman the news photographer back there about two blocks. Let's go get him."

They were back in about three minutes. I hunched down even farther and listened while the photographer and the two policemen talked.

"I've got just the caption," one voice said. "Monkey drives auto across continent."

"I wonder what the actual story is?" the newsman asked. "That monkey looks like the one that belongs to Old Char-lie."

I decided it was time to show myself, because I didn't want to get blamed for kidnaping a monkey. I sat up and explained what had happened. Diego still had the earring in his fist, and it was clenched as tightly as ever.

"My advice is to go buy the shiniest, gaudiest cheap earring you can find," the newsman said. "He'll probably trade."

"That makes sense," one of the officers said. "Meanwhile we'll see if we can locate Old Charlie. He's often over at Louie's Diner."

They started to drive off and then paused. The officer on the right leaned out the window and called, "Don't leave the key in the ignition. That monkey is smarter than you think!"

I got out, leaving Diego alone, and went to hunt for Mrs. Glass. I found her halfway down Olvera Street. It was no trick to locate some cheap earrings, as there were stands full of costume jewelry. We picked a flashy, dangly pair and hurried back to the car. As we got near, we saw a man peering in the window. When he straightened up, we discovered it was Mr. Glass. He turned around and saw us just as we recognized him.

"No!" he exploded. "This is too much. Parakeets, pine cones, and now a monkey! I will not travel across the country with a monkey in the car! I don't care whose he is or where you got him—he's got to go!"

"Give us a chance to explain," Mrs. Glass said. "We don't want to take him anywhere. I'm merely trying to get my earring back."

I got in the car with Diego and offered him one of the new earrings. He was quite pleased and promptly took it in his left hand. Then I offered him the second one. He hesitated a minute, making up his mind.

Finally he opened his fingers, let Mrs. Glass's earring drop, and took the new one. Mr. Glass had calmed down by this time and was watching with Midge and her mother through the window.

"Fine work, Henry," Mrs. Glass said, giving a sigh of relief as I handed her the earring.

"You can see what that monkey thinks of your taste in

earrings," Mr. Glass said with a chuckle. "He prefers those ten-cent ones to yours."

Mrs. Glass was a little annoyed at all the trouble. "That's right," she said. "He thinks the same of *your* taste in earrings. You gave these to me on our honeymoon. That's why I was so anxious to get them back."

Thursday, June 24th—Las Vegas, Nevada

Las Vegas and the whole state of Nevada are a big disappointment. There are no fireworks. It doesn't make sense. They'll let you lose a fortune gambling, but you can't spend ten cents on cherry bombs. This is the state where they set off atom bombs, but firecrackers are out.

I feel that we are headed across the continent at last. Right now I am sitting beside the swimming pool at our motel. Sitting beside a swimming pool is about the only place to be sitting in Las Vegas unless you are inside an air-conditioned restaurant.

Both Midge and I were in the water so long that we were getting waterlogged. She's sun bathing, and I decided to write in my journal. I don't get very tan—I just peel, especially my nose. This is a swank pool with umbrellas, and tables, and chaise longues to lie on. I'm not sure about that word, and I don't have a dictionary along. Anyhow, they have those half-couches with one end that you can raise or lower. The motel is very modern and expensive-looking, and I'm sitting here beside the pool pretending I'm rich. I think I'll have Midge take my picture. It will be fun someday remembering how I feel now.

Midge is wearing dark glasses, and she says she's pretending to be a movie starlet going incognito. She has real nerve even to mention movie stars after yesterday. The true reason she is wearing dark glasses is that she has a black eye.

Mr. and Mrs. Glass are still asleep. After leaving Disneyland last night, we drove on across the desert and didn't arrive here until the small hours of the morning. There isn't much to tell about the desert except that it's hot even in the middle of the night. I would like to have seen more of the desert, but it was dark, and there wasn't much point to staying awake. Midge and I slept a good part of the way, which is why we are up and around.

No matter when you arrive in Las Vegas it's blazing with lights, it seems. Mr. Glass says it is seventy-five per cent motels, twenty per cent night clubs and gambling casinos, and four per cent restaurants, with one per cent left for service stations and drugstores. I haven't seen the drug-store yet.

Yesterday, after we said good-by to Diego, we drove out to Anaheim, which is where Disneyland is located. We parked our car in an enormous parking lot and walked over to the main entrance. I don't know how to describe Disneyland except to say that it's as much fun as I've always heard it is. Mr. Glass bought each of us a book of tickets, and by the time we had used those, we'd seen about everything, and we were really tired.

I won't describe any of the details of Disneyland, because you can get folders with maps and colored pictures; you can read about it in the magazines; and I suppose almost everyone has seen parts of it on TV. We went on rides in boats, old-fashioned trains, canoes, bobsleds, suspension cable cars, pack mules, and steamboats. We visited all sorts of exhibits, shot rifles at the shooting galleries, and ate all sorts of things. Disneyland has about everything you could ask for except firecrackers. Main Street is supposed to look like a small American town in 1900, and I was certain the stores would have firecrackers, but they didn't.

"We've got a license to scare you to death, to shoot hundreds of Indians and outlaws every day, and to sell you concoctions that will probably ruin your digestion for life, but we can't sell you firecrackers," a man told me.

Mr. and Mrs. Glass stayed only an hour. Mr. Glass had an old friend from his Navy days living only five miles away. We were all invited to dinner, but naturally Midge and I preferred to stay at Disneyland. We promised to be just outside the main gate at nine-thirty.

"You're both responsible young people," Mrs. Glass said as she left. "If you have any doubts about where you are or how to get back to the main gate, ask any of the young men in uniform. Remember, as long as you stay inside Disneyland, and behave yourselves, nothing can happen."

"I'm not so sure," Mr. Glass said. "Only what does happen will be to Disneyland. I'm beginning to understand what Al meant. Both of these children affect the stars. Maybe we ought to warn Walt."

"Do you know Walt Disney?" I asked.

"No, but I probably will," Mr. Glass said. "Remember, Midge, you can't take Disneyland or any part of it home in the car. Anything you buy in the way of souvenirs has to go in that purse of yours."

I've become used to being kidded about strange things happening when I'm around, but I honestly don't see why Mr. Glass feels that way. We haven't had any accidents, nothing's been stolen, and there hasn't been even a flat tire so far. We'd spent the day in Los Angeles, and there wasn't any earthquake. If anything unusual is going to happen, it should happen in Los Angeles.

We had walked around enough with Mr. and Mrs. Glass to know what we wanted to do, so after we had said good-by to them, we set out to go on all the important rides.

Midge certainly enjoyed Disneyland, and she let every-one know it. There is a ride called a bobsled run. You zip up and down through an imitation mountain called the "Matterhorn." Sometimes you're halfway down a steep slope and your stomach is fifteen feet above you. During most of the ride you could hear Midge screaming for miles. I thought it was exciting, too, but of course I didn't scream. Men are naturally more dignified than women.

We were having a good time, but a perfectly normal one, until we rode the Skyway. The Skyway is a suspension cable car ride from Fantasyland to Tomorrowland. Little round cars hang from cables, and you ride high above the people, above a lagoon, and right through the mountain with the bobsled ride. While you ride one way, other peo-ple are riding in the opposite direction on another cable about ten feet away. Midge and I were in a car about mid-way in the ride when she got very excited about the car on the other cable. I was trying to watch the submarine in the lagoon below when she poked me.

"Hank, that man in the car is looking at me!"

"So?" I asked, not much interested. I did glance at him, but all I saw was a young man about twenty to twenty-five years old with sun-bleached blond hair and a pair of dark glasses.

"He's been staring at me," Midge insisted. "I happened to look at him when the car was still up ahead, and he's been looking at me ever since."

I looked at Midge closely but I didn't see anything peculiar about her. She was wearing a skirt and a blouse and had her hair in a pony tail. Midge is not especially pretty, but she's cute and perfectly normal-looking.

"Don't worry, you look all right," I told her. "There's a smudge of dirt on your forehead, but there's nothing else wrong."

By this time the car had passed and was getting farther away by the second.

"Look, he's turning around to look at me!" she said, bouncing so much that I was afraid the trolley might bounce off the cable.

"How do you know he's looking at you?" I asked. "Maybe he's looking back at the Matterhorn or at the submarine. Or maybe even me."

"At you!" she said. "Why would he look at you?"

"I don't know," I said. "I can't see any reason why he would want to look at either of us. With those dark glasses, there's no way of knowing what he's looking at."

"Well, he looked at me," Midge said. "And I think I know why."

Midge isn't silly like most girls. Usually she has more sense than to think the whole world is looking at her, but I guess this was one of her off days. This man was wearing a pair of those huge dark glasses, and I don't know how she could be certain he even had eyes.

"All right, why was he looking at you?" I asked.

"That was Tab Hunter."

"Who's he?"

"Who's he?" She gasped. "Why, he's just one of the most famous movie stars who ever lived."

I've lived most of my life abroad, and so I suppose I'm way behind on movie stars. I probably wouldn't have known what he looked like even if I had been in the United States all the time, because I'm not much interested in gushy, romantic pictures, and from what Midge tells me he is usually in that kind.

"I won't argue," I told her. "We'll agree Tab Hunter is famous. What makes you think that was him?"

"Because I'd know Tab Hunter anywhere," Midge said, sighing like a sick calf. "The reason he's wearing those dark glasses is that he doesn't want people to recognize him and bother him. Why, he'd be mobbed if people realized who he was!"

"What did he come to Disneyland for if he's avoiding people?" I wanted to know. "I'd think he'd expect to find a few in a place like this."

"I think he's looking for someone," she said, very mysteriously. "Like me."

"Why would he be looking for you? Does he know your family?"

"No, silly! I read in a magazine the other day that he is going to be in a movie and one of the important characters will be a girl about my age. I think he is out here looking for someone to fit the part. What would be more sensible than to look in Disneyland, where he'd see thousands of girls my age?"

I don't know much about making movies, but I think the director or producer or someone like that picks the people for different parts. Even if one actor does pick the other actors, I couldn't see why he would be riding high above Disneyland in a cable car looking for a girl actress. All he could see from there would be the tops of their heads. I told Midge this, but it didn't make any impression. When a girl gets movie-struck, nothing makes sense.

"Look at all these people," she wailed as we got off the car. "How will he ever find me again?"

"What difference does it make?" I asked. "With all these people he won't have any trouble finding hundreds of girls who'll fit the part."

That seemed to be the wrong thing to say, because it only made her more excited. Nothing would do but to hurry back to where we had got on the Skyway. The simplest method would have been to ride back, but there was a long line waiting. Trying to hurry through Disneyland is like trying to swim rapidly up a fast stream. When we got back to the spot where we had started, he had disappeared.

For the next half-hour we wandered around aimlessly. I tried to get Midge to go in several places, but all she wanted to do was to stare at people who went by. Since there is no scarcity of people in Disneyland, she was really busy. I imagine her neck finally got tired, twisting this way and that, because she agreed to go for a ride on the Mule Train in Frontierland.

The Mule Train is a string of eight or nine burros with saddles. Each burro is tied to the one ahead, and the front burro is ridden by a guide. You wind across a make-believe desert and around some trails. We were riding along one of these trails, fairly high above the park, when suddenly Midge thought she spotted her man. She got very excited and stood up in the stirrups. I was riding on the burro right behind her.

"How can I get out of here quick?" she asked, turning around.

"You can't," I told her.

"I have to!"

Since very little kids ride the burros, I suppose they are picked to be very gentle and they are well trained. Maybe Midge's burro thought she was falling off, or maybe he didn't like her and decided to be stubborn. Anyhow, he suddenly stopped in his tracks. Naturally that stopped my burro and the two behind me. The ones ahead tugged half-heartedly and then stopped too.

"Come on, move, you stubborn idiot!" Midge said, kicking her burro with her heels.

She might as well not have been on his back for all the attention the animal paid to her. The guide at the head of the line had to come back, coax, threaten, and use a stick before we finally got moving again. He looked crossly at both Midge and the burro, which is only half what they deserved. Altogether the delay lasted about five minutes, and the man she saw, or thought she saw, was nowhere around when we got back to the starting point. Midge was furious, but there was nothing she could do about it.

She gradually returned to normal and even began to act interested in what we were doing. Then we took what I think is the best ride in Disneyland, a trip by boat through Adventureland's jungle. There were huge trees, hanging vines, and all sorts of tropical foliage. Spotted through the jungle were elephants, crocodiles, lions, tigers, and other animals. They were all fakes, but many of them were animated, and they looked real. The villages of head-hunters were filled with actual people made up to look like savages. You could hear roars and growls and native chants as you glided along, and you had the feeling of actually being in a tropical jungle.

I have always been very interested in animals, and I was so busy looking around me that I didn't pay much attention to the people in the boat. We were seated on the right side about halfway between the bow and the stern. There was a break in the rail at that point, and so I was able to lean out and see ahead. In my travel book I'll advise everyone to get a seat near the bow. That way you can see the different animals sooner than the other passengers.

Midge was seated beside me, but since the seat was along the side of the boat, and I was twisted around facing the bow, she was really behind me, and I didn't know what she was doing. I supposed she was as interested in the tour as I was, but I was mistaken. I can't imagine anyone wasting time looking at people when he can look at crocodiles or hippopotamuses, but that's what Midge was doing. At one point in the twisting, turning canal or river, you can see across a very narrow strip. There was another boat not far behind us, and it passed this spot just as we did. Midge apparently was looking at it instead of the sights our guide was talking about. As the two boats passed, the people could see each other clearly and Midge saw the man she claimed was Tab Hunter. She told me later that he saw her and waved, and possibly he did. I don't know what happened, because at this point a hippopotamus came up out of the water almost directly ahead. It opened its mouth wide enough to swallow a cow and came right at us. I knew it was a fake, but still it was scary. The guide pretended it was alive, and he was very convincing. He picked up a gun, pointed it at the hippo, and fired. It sounded like both barrels of a double-barreled shotgun going off at one time. Everyone was looking straight at the hippo, I guess, except Midge. She was up on her knees and was leaning out trying to see the boat behind us, which was rounding a curve and coming into view. Several people let out screams when the gun went off. Midge, who wasn't paying any attention, was even more startled. She gave a yelp, grabbed at the post that supported the canopy, swung around, bumped into my elbow, and then went over the side with a splash.

A stout middle-aged woman was sitting right behind Midge. She tried to grab Midge's leg but she was too slow. She wasn't slow in shouting an alarm, however.

"She fell overboard!" she started screaming. "Help, help! The little girl fell in!"

You never heard such a racket. Some of those people must have thought the hippo was real, because several started screaming that it would get her or the crocodiles

would. Actually there wasn't any danger at all. The water wasn't deep, and besides, Midge is a good swimmer. They stopped the boat immediately, and several of us leaned over and pulled her in. Everyone crowded around to find out if she was all right.

"I'm just wet, that's all," Midge said. "And I bumped my eye on Henry's elbow."

She looked a bedraggled mess. That water wasn't the cleanest in the world. Her pony tail dripped water, and her blouse hung on her like a feed sack. Midge is a skinny girl, anyhow, and when wet she looked like a scarecrow.

When we got back to the dock several attendants clustered around her, wanting to know if she was all right. They insisted on taking her over to a first-aid station. As we were leaving, the boat behind ours docked, and a tall man with blond hair rushed over to us. Midge was right, it was the same man we had seen on the Skyway. She didn't want to see him now that she looked like a wet dish towel, so she pretended not to notice.

"Is she all right?" he asked.

"She's fine," one of the attendants assured him.

"Aren't you Margaret Glass?" he asked.

Midge had to turn around. She tried to smile sweetly and managed to look like a half-drowned puppy.

"Yes, I'm Margaret Glass."

"Well, I'm Carter Brown," he said. "I gave you tennis lessons last summer, do you remember? In Princeton, New Jersey."

"I didn't recognize you because of the dark glasses," Midge said weakly. "Sure I remember."

"I'm sort of homesick for New Jersey," Mr. Brown said, walking beside us. "I've been out here about ten months now. It's nice seeing an old friend. Is there anything I can do for you, Margaret? Can I find your parents for you and ask them to get you some dry clothes?"

There wasn't anything that needed to be done that Disneyland wasn't prepared to do. They even have a baby station where mothers can feed babies, change their diapers, and warm bottles. Midge got all cleaned up and combed her hair. She got her clothes rinsed out and dried, and although she had an un-ironed look, she was fairly respectable when she came out about thirty minutes later.

"I'm as good as new," she said, grinning. "Except for my eye. You would have to stick that bony elbow of yours right in my eye."

Her eye was already beginning to get puffy, and today it is a dirty purplish brown.

"Carter Brown went on," I told her. "He said to say hello to your parents."

"I'd like to get even with him," Midge said. "What right has he got going around looking so much like Tab Hunter?"

I didn't say anything, but that remark shows how unreasonable girls can be. Carter Brown was just trying to be friendly. How could he help it if she was silly enough to think he was a movie star?

Friday, June 25th—Herman's Gulch, Arizona

Arizona doesn't sell firecrackers. Otherwise it's an interesting state, and I wouldn't mind living here.

We spent yesterday loafing in Las Vegas. Last night Mr. and Mrs. Glass went out to a night club. They wouldn't take us along, but we got to go to a movie. This morning Mr. and Mrs. Glass slept late while Midge and I went swimming again. We didn't drive very far today. It was one o'clock by the time we left Las Vegas and we arrived at our motel here in Herman's Gulch about seven.

Herman's Gulch is having a big celebration tomorrow in honor of the seventy-fifth anniversary of the saving of the settlement by a little Indian girl. Actually the anniversary was Wednesday, but they are celebrating tomorrow because it will be a Saturday. Mr. Glass read about it someplace and made reservations weeks and weeks ago.

Herman's Gulch isn't a very big town, but it is certainly jumping tonight. Tomorrow they expect thousands of people at the celebration, driving in from Phoenix, Flagstaff, and places like that. And of course there are already a lot of people here. The motels are all full, and there are trailers everywhere.

There will be a rodeo, a big parade, speeches, Indian dances, fireworks, and all sorts of races and contests. There is a long list of prizes, and they aren't small ones either. Mr. Glass looked at the poster, whistled, and said he wouldn't be surprised if the total was more than the yearly budget for the entire state. The two biggest prizes are for the cowboy winning the most points at the rodeo and for the best float in the parade. These are each seven hundred and fifty dollars. Earlier this evening while we were walking around we learned that the reason they are able to offer such big prizes is that the celebration has an endowment fund. A rich prospector by the name of Adolph Ullman prospected in the area for years. When he wasn't out in the desert with his burro Hannah, he lived in Herman's Gulch. When he died he left a sizable fortune to the town with directions that part of it was for the annual celebration and part for a library. The library was to be named after his burro Hannah. We walked around to look at the library. It was closed, but from the outside it looked very nice. It was called "The Hannah Memorial Library," and there was a stone statue of a burro out in front. The man who gave us all the information said that old Adolph had always enjoyed the annual celebration, and so they weren't too surprised when he left some money for it. However, he had never been known to read a book, and most people doubted if he could read.

"A lot of folks claim that Hannah could read and that's why he said the library was to be named after her," he told us. "I doubt that, although that burro was smarter in many ways than old Adolph."

"What happened to her?" Midge asked.

"He left money to take care of her for the rest of her life. In fact she had a little stable back of the library. Lived better than most people in Herman's Gulch until she died about ten years ago."

This afternoon, about twenty-five miles outside Herman's Gulch we met a group of Hopi Indians who are entering the float contest tomorrow. We saw them again this evening after dinner. They are certainly working hard, and we'll be rooting for them tomorrow.

We met them in an odd way. We were driving along the highway, which was a hot, dusty road, as all the roads are here, when we came up behind a dilapidated old Packard sedan pulling an enormous trailer. Just ahead of the sedan was an old truck. Both were piled high with all sorts of bundles and boxes and bags. They were traveling about thirty miles an hour, but even at that speed the trailer wobbled back and forth.

"Look at that rig," Mr. Glass said. "That trailer isn't balanced right, that's why it sways that way. They'll wear out their tires in no time."

We had driven for miles without meeting more than an occasional car but now that we wanted to pass this procession, there was a long string of traffic from the opposite direction. We poked along behind the trailer, getting hotter and more annoyed by the minute. Finally the road appeared to be clear, and we were pulling out to pass when a bundle came untied from the trailer and fell off, landing right in front of the car. Mr. Glass had no idea what was in it, so he slammed on the brakes and swerved. We managed to miss the bundle but almost went in the ditch.

"That was good driving," Mrs. Glass said.

Mr. Glass was mad. He got out and looked at the tire marks on the pavement and said, "There's about ten dollars' worth of rubber back there. We come within inches of a dangerous accident, and they don't even know anything's happened."

The truck and sedan were half a mile ahead by this time, completely unaware that they had lost anything.

"What's in the bundle?" Mrs. Glass asked.

Midge and I hurried back to the bundle. It was an old canvas garment bag with a zipper. We unzipped it, and inside we saw some of the most beautiful headdresses I have ever seen. Some were the usual Indian headdresses of feathers, and others were combinations of fur and feathers. They were brightly colored and decorated with fancy beadwork. We took a quick look at them and then picked up the bundle and hurried to the car.

Mrs. Glass looked at them and said, "Those must be valuable. We'll have to catch that car, Ernie."

"I don't know that I want to try," Mr. Glass said. "They might drop something else, and this time we might not be so lucky."

Mr. Glass does a lot of grumbling that doesn't mean

much, because as soon as we stuck the bundle in the car and got in ourselves, he started off and in no time was going about sixty-five or seventy miles an hour. A few minutes later we were behind the Indians again. This time the road was clear, and we were able to pull up alongside their car. I opened the window and tried to tell them what had happened but the noise of the car and the wind was too much. Finally, by motioning for them to pull over to the side of the road, we got them to stop. The truck kept on for a short distance, and then the driver noticed what had happened, and he stopped too.

More people piled out of that car and truck than I thought was possible. Mr. Glass said later that he thought they had a balcony in the big Packard, but I don't see how they could have. They were just wedged in, and on a hot day that must have been pretty uncomfortable. The one in charge was a big, heavy gray-headed Indian. He walked halfway from the sedan to our station wagon and then waited for Mr. Glass to meet him. Naturally, Midge and I were right beside Mr. Glass.

"A bundle dropped off your trailer," Mr. Glass explained. "It's full of headdresses, I think. We thought you might want it."

Everybody began talking at once until the big Indian in charge quieted them. He held up his hand, and they all stopped talking immediately. "I am Bald Eagle, Chief of the Snake Clan of the Hopi Indians. We thank you very much. Those are our ceremonial headdresses."

106

They couldn't have been more grateful. Mr. Glass didn't say a thing about our almost having had an accident. Altogether we had quite a powwow beside the road with all the Indians saying how much they appreciated our returning the headdresses and Mr. and Mrs. Glass saying it was nothing. The headdresses were not only semisacred; they were needed for the big parade in the celebration in Herman's Gulch. There were fourteen Indians altogether, and all of them were older boys or men except one elderly Indian woman and one fat-faced girl about Midge's age. Chief Bald Eagle took a fancy to Midge and said she looked like his granddaughter Flying Antelope.

"Where is your granddaughter?" Midge asked.

"She's a big girl now," Bald Eagle said. "She's going to school."

"What grade is she in?" Midge asked.

"Third year," said Bald Eagle. "At Vassar. She has what you call a scholarship."

After another round of thanks, we piled back into our cars and all set off again for Herman's Gulch. This evening as we were walking around after dinner we saw their camp. They had a big canvas screen around their trailer, and I guess they were getting it ready for the parade. Mr. Glass said he thinks the sides fold out, making a big platform for a float. Several of the braves were standing guard, and the rest were inside the screen working. Chief Bald Eagle squatted beside a small fire, stirring something in a pot and mumbling to himself.

On our way back to the motel we saw the old Indian woman and the fat-faced little girl. They were in an open-front stand that sold hot tamales, chili, and hot dogs. Both were busily eating, and the little fat-faced girl's cheeks were bulging, she was eating so fast.

"If they eat much of that hot Mexican food, they'll be sorry tomorrow," Mr. Glass said. "I know from experience."

"I imagine they're used to it," Mrs. Glass said. "Indians are supposed to have very strong stomachs."

Sunday, June 27th—Herman's Gulch, Arizona

I'm writing this before breakfast. As soon as everybody's awake and we've eaten, we'll be on our way to the Grand Canyon.

The celebration was yesterday, and it was quite a day. I don't know when I've had more fun, and Midge, I'm sure, will agree.

The rodeo was the most exciting I've ever seen; the games and contests were all very interesting; and the parade was wonderful. Midge and I were both in it, and to top everything off, we are now Hopi Indians. We had a full-fledged ceremony last night and were adopted into the tribe. My name is Little Wolf and Midge's is Desert Rose. We even look like Indians.

The celebration started early. By nine o'clock the town was jammed with people; all the food stands were in operation, and, according to Mr. Glass, the place looked like an old-fashioned county fair in Kansas. We were slow in getting up, and by the time we got dressed and downtown, we couldn't get in either of the town's two restaurants. That didn't bother Midge or me much, because there were hot-dog stands all over. We had hamburgers and lemonade for breakfast, but Mr. and Mrs.

Glass insisted on going from place to place until they finally got a cup of hot coffee.

We were wandering around about ten-thirty when Chief Bald Eagle came hurrying up. "Ah, my white friends," he said, taking off his old cowboy hat and bowing, "I have been looking all over for you. I asked at the motel, but you weren't there. We need your help."

"What for?" Mr. Glass asked.

"Our little girl, Sleeping Turtle, ate something she shouldn't last night. Now she is very sick."

"See, I was right," Mr. Glass said triumphantly.

"Right about what?" Bald Eagle asked.

"I saw her eating hot tamales and some other Mexican food," Mr. Glass told him. "That stuff will give you a king-sized tummy ache plus making you stay close to a rest room for a day or two. It's not serious, though. She'll be all right tomorrow."

"If she's very sick, you'd best find a doctor," Mrs. Glass advised. "We couldn't help you."

"Sleeping Turtle will be all right," said the Chief with a wave of his hand. "The reason we need help is that she is too sick to be in the parade. She's the only little girl we have."

"I still don't understand," Mrs. Glass said.

"We want to borrow your little girl," Bald Eagle explained. "She will have a part of great honor. She is the little Indian princess who saves the town."

"That sounds like fun," Midge said, all for the idea

immediately. "I've never been on a float in a parade."

She put two fingers behind her head and began dancing around in a circle chanting, "I'm Minnehaha, the Indian princess."

"Be quiet, and behave yourself!" Mrs. Glass said. "I'm not sure, Chief Bald Eagle. I'd like to know more about what you want her to do."

Bald Eagle looked around suspiciously and then pulled us off to one side. "I don't want anyone to know until the last minute what we have planned for our float. What I tell you must be kept secret. There are other Indians from other villages who would like to know, so they could steal our idea. And whites too. I don't trust them either. Some people would do anything to win the prize."

"You can trust us," Mr. Glass assured him. "We're completely neutral in this cowboy and Indian struggle."

"Many years ago when Herman's Gulch was a tiny settlement, the Navajos decided one night to attack it, kill all the men, burn the houses, and carry off the women." Chief Bald Eagle was a good actor. He paused, drew his knife out of its sheath, and waved it slowly across his face. Then his fierce expression changed, and he smiled until all six of his teeth showed.

"Those were the treacherous Navajos. The Hopis were peace-loving Indians. Anyhow, while the Navajos were having their war dance and making their plans, a little Indian princess, Desert Rose, slipped away in the dark and rode all the rest of the night to warn the settlement."

Bald Eagle paused again, drew himself up, and stuck out his chest. "It is not well known, but Desert Rose's mother was a Hopi, so she had the noble thoughts of a Hopi."

He lowered his voice to barely more than a whisper. "Our float will show the Navajo camp with the braves around the campfire planning the attack. The little Indian princess is slipping away and climbing onto her horse."

Just thinking about the float made Bald Eagle excited. "We have worked months on the scene. Every bit of it is perfect and beautiful. The float will be magnificent!" He looked dejected. "But now we have no little princess unless you help us."

"Well," said Mrs. Glass doubtfully. "How long would it take?"

"If she can come with me now, Sleeping Turtle's mother will get her dressed and ready. We have to be in line by twelve-thirty."

It was a few minutes past eleven by this time. I could tell from Mrs. Glass's face that she wasn't enthusiastic about letting Midge go off by herself, even with the noble and trustworthy Hopis. Midge was a little doubtful too, but the idea of being an Indian princess appealed to her.

"Could you take Henry too?" Midge asked. "He could be an Indian brave."

Bald Eagle was rather insulting the way he looked at me. Then he reached out and took off my glasses. "He looks a little scrawny for a Hopi," he said, "but he'll do."

Mr. and Mrs. Glass went with us to the camp. Bald

Eagle looked around carefully and finally led us through an opening in the canvas screen. The float was beautiful. They must have spent a great deal of time on it. In one corner was an Indian hut made of mud and sticks with a little dog tied in front. In the center of the float was a campfire all ready to light. There were a kettle and a few Indian pots, and the entire bed of the float had been covered with dirt and rocks so that it looked like part of the desert. A Joshua tree, a cactus, and several other desert plants looked as though they were actually growing from the desert. There were several lizards, a road runner, and two rattlesnakes scattered here and there. They were motionless, so I suppose they were stuffed, but they looked so natural I didn't try touching the snakes.

At the opposite corner from the hut was a wooden horse that had probably been on a merry-go-round at one time. It had been repainted and was a pinto now. On its back was a frayed Indian blanket.

"The little princess stands beside the pony, ready to jump on its back and ride away," Chief Bald Eagle said proudly. "And when the braves in their war dress are gathered around the campfire, it will look much better."

The float was a work of art as it was. Mrs. Glass was quite impressed. "I guess it will be all right," she said finally. "We'll leave the children here, and we'll go get them something for lunch and be back."

"We'll give them something to eat," Bald Eagle assured her.

"I know you will," Mrs. Glass said. "But you know what happened to Sleeping Turtle when she ate food last night that she wasn't used to eating. We don't want your substitute princess to get sick because she isn't used to your food."

"That's right," Bald Eagle agreed.

As soon as Mr. and Mrs. Glass had left, Bald Eagle called everyone together and explained that we were to be part of the float. "The little girl looks just like my granddaughter Flying Antelope. The time that Flying Antelope was part of our float, we won the prize. It is a good omen. Now the first thing we have to do is turn them from palefaces into Hopis."

Two Indian boys led me over to a little tent. A few minutes later a third one came in with a potful of dirty brown stuff.

"Take off your clothes and rub this all over," one of them told me. "It'll make you brown."

I guess I didn't look very enthusiastic.

"It is harmless," he told me. "It's made from the bark of a tree."

They gave me a cloth and in a few minutes I really had a tan. Whatever the stain was, it was powerful.

"What if I get hot during the parade and sweat starts running down my face?" I asked one of the boys. "Won't I streak?"

"Water won't wash it off," he said confidently.

"How do I get it off after the parade?" I asked.

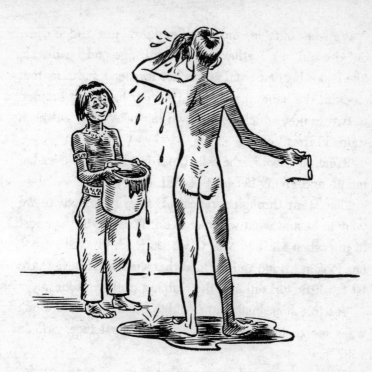

"You don't," he said with a grin. "You're an Indian for at least a week. It'll wear off in time."

After I was all stained I got dressed in Indian moccasins with fur cuffs, an Indian breechcloth, and a red-fringed jacket decorated with beads. All I kept of my own was my underwear shorts. The Indian clothes didn't look as though they had been washed too recently, but I decided it was too late to complain. They fitted me with a head-dress but then took that off.

"Wait until the parade starts," they told me. "It's too hot and heavy now."

We went outside, and a few minutes later Midge came out dressed in a leather dress with fringe and beadwork. She had a beaded band across her forehead and a feather stuck in the band at the rear. Her hair had been braided in two braids, which hung down her back. She had been stained brown too.

"How do I look?" she asked, putting her hand over her mouth and giving her idea of an Indian yell.

They went through a rehearsal, showing us where we were to be and what we were to do. We were in the midst of this when Mr. and Mrs. Glass returned. Mrs. Glass took one look at Midge and decided that she should never have let her little girl fall into the clutches of the redskins.

"It's just some make-up," Midge explained. "You don't want me to look like an anemic little paleface girl, do you?"

We ate our sandwiches, and then it was time to start for the parade. We all took our places, the canvas screen was removed, and off we went, pulled by the old Packard sedan. Chief Bald Eagle was driving. Sleeping Turtle stayed in camp with her stomach-ache, and her mother stayed to take care of her. All the rest of us, including Midge, were on the float.

I didn't have much to do except sit around the campfire and look wise. I think I did a good job of that even without my glasses. Every few minutes one of the braves would jump up, chant something, beat his chest, and do a little war dance. Since I didn't know the Hopi language or their dances, I sat and said, "Ugh." I'll bet I said, "Ugh" in more different ways then any Indian ever did.

Midge was in her glory. At the last minute it was decided that she should actually be riding the horse instead of being about to mount. She looked very pretty in her Indian costume with all its bright beadwork. The more the crowd cheered, the more she beamed. She smiled at everyone, waved, and blew kisses. Once she almost gave away the secret that she wasn't an Indian. There was a man at one corner with a large motion-picture camera.

Midge turned around and said, "Smile, everyone, you're on TV."

There were three bands in the parade, four marching groups, a group of drum majorettes, dozens upon dozens of horses, and twenty-eight floats. We went up and down every street in town, but since it was a small town, that didn't take long. The reviewing stand, where the mayor and the judges sat, was in front of the library, right beside the statue of Hannah the burro.

Riding on the float was a lot of fun, but we didn't get a chance to see much of the rest of the parade the way you do when you are a spectator. After it was over, we all jumped off to go up and down the line to look at our competition. The trouble was that everyone else did the same thing, and you really can't get a good idea of a float with all the people missing, unless it's the kind that has no people.

We had to wait only ten minutes to learn the results. Even though I was certain we had the best float, it was a thrill when it was announced that we had won. Midge let out a whoop that they must have heard back in the Hopi village, wherever that was. Bald Eagle was smiles all over, and the braves all did a dance.

We had to go back with the winning band and the winning horses of each class to be present for the official announcement. When the mayor came to us he made quite a little speech.

"We are happy to award float eighteen the first prize.

We picked it because of the originality of its theme, the close attention to detail, and above all its authenticity. As Chief Bald Eagle stated in his entry blank, this float is an authentic Hopi Indian production. Every detail about it is authentic, from the rattlesnake to the costumes. And of course we don't need to say that the actors on the float are authentic Hopi Indians. As you all know, the float represents the dramatic warning by the little Indian princess of the planned Indian attack on the settlement. Had it not been for this brave little girl, Herman's Gulch might not be in existence today. We are happy to award the first prize to the Snake Clan of the Hopi Indian tribe. Their float is a symbol of the close cooperation and accord that now exists between the red man and the white man."

"This float represents a lot of cooperation on the part of a white girl and boy too," Midge said to me over her shoulder.

It was about two o'clock by the time we got back to the Hopis' camp and were able to shift back into our own clothes. The Indians were all very happy and should have been, since they won seven hundred and fifty dollars. Bald Eagle gave Midge a silver ring with a beautiful turquoise stone and gave me a wonderful silver belt buckle with a turquoise stone in the center.

"Tonight we are having Indian dances, and we want you to come as our honored guests," he told us. "The dances will start after it gets dark."

After leaving the Hopi camp, we went to the rodeo, which was the best rodeo I've ever seen. Of course I've seen only two, but Mr. Glass has seen quite a few, and he said this was one of the best. The cowboys rode bucking broncos and steers, and there were all sorts of roping and bulldogging contests. We saw several races and visited a number of stands before six o'clock. Then we went back to the motel to wash off some of the dust before going out for dinner. Midge and I decided to take a swim. When I got into my trunks there was only a small streak of white showing below the legs of my shorts as I had been stained all over. Aside from being very dark, I guess I looked reasonably normal.

Midge and her mother were in the adjoining room. I guess Mrs. Glass was lying on the bed resting and probably had her eyes closed. I heard Midge giggling, and then she called to me. "Henry, wait until you see me in my bathing suit. I look like I had leprosy or some strange disease."

Mrs. Glass must have opened her eyes because I heard her say, "Margaret Glass, don't you dare leave this room looking like that! You get right back in the bathroom and take a shower and scrub that stuff off."

"It won't wash off," Midge said. "I just tried with a face cloth and soap."

"Won't wash off!" Mrs. Glass said, almost shrieking. "What do you mean, it won't wash off?"

"Me redskin for good," Midge said, giggling. "It won't

come off. Henry, will that brown stuff come off you?"

There was nothing to do but admit Midge was right and that the Indians had told me it had to wear off. Mrs. Glass almost blew her top, and it was a good thing Chief Bald Eagle wasn't around, because there would have been war again between the white man and the red man.

Midge opened the connecting door, and I have to admit she was a strange sight. Since she had been wearing an Indian dress, they had only stained her face and the parts of her arms and legs that showed. Her arms up to her shoulders were stained, and her face and neck, and her legs up to just above the knees. She has very white skin, and she certainly looked like a freak, half brown and half white.

"If that stuff is such a powerful stain it might be poisonous," Mrs. Glass said.

"No, they said it was harmless," I told her.

"Well, Chief Bald Eagle can just give us some more so that Margaret can at least make herself one shade. I won't have her going around in shorts until she is. Swimming while she looks like that is simply out of the question."

I guess you can't stay at the boiling point indefinitely, and Mrs. Glass gradually simmered down. Things were about normal again when there was a knock on our door. It was Chief Bald Eagle. I don't know whether it was an accident or whether he saw that something was wrong, but before Mrs. Glass could really get going, Bald Eagle stopped her.

"I want to apologize for this afternoon. In all the excitement of winning the first prize, I forgot where I had put my gift for the lady. Now I've found it, and I want to give it to you with the thanks of the Snake Clan."

He pulled out a beautiful turquoise and silver pin and handed it to Mrs. Glass with a flourish. It was like sticking a balloon with a pin. About all she could do was say, "Thank you," and ask for some more stain to make Midge all one color.

"I'll send some immediately," Chief Bald Eagle promised. "I have another favor to ask. We would like the little girl and the boy to come early to our dances tonight. We want to have a special ceremony and adopt them into our tribe."

"I'm sure that would be a great honor," Mrs. Glass said, trying to hedge. "But are you certain you want to? After all, you know very little about them, and we will be leaving tomorrow."

"We would be proud to have them as Hopis," Bald Eagle said. "Besides, it might save a little trouble. It's better to be safe than sorry."

"What do you mean?" Mrs. Glass asked. "What sort of trouble?"

Bald Eagle looked uncomfortable. "When I filled out our entry blank for the float contest some weeks ago, I said that everything in our float was authentic Hopi. The judges mentioned that. At that time I expected to have Sleeping Turtle as the Indian princess, and I told the truth. The float that won second place had two Zuñi Indians in it. I have heard whispers that they suspect not everyone on the float was a real Hopi and may claim we won by fraud."

"I don't see how that could make any difference," Mrs. Glass said. "The second-place float had two Indians and I think four whites. Most of the others were white."

"I know," Bald Eagle agreed, "but they didn't claim to be anything they weren't. I don't think we could be disqualified, but just to be safe, it would be wise to adopt the boy and girl. Then if any questions are asked, we can speak without fear. As everyone knows, a Hopi speaks only the truth."

"I'd like to know a little about what this adoption ceremony involves," Mrs. Glass said. "I don't want Margaret to be stained some other color, or to have her head shaved, or anything like that. I happen to like her the way she was before we got involved in all this."

"The ceremony is very simple," Bald Eagle said. "It will have to be a very short one as we haven't time for a full adoption ceremony."

It was finally agreed, and at seven-thirty we went over to the Hopi camp. I won't go into a long description of the full ceremony, but they did a lot of dancing and singing, and Chief Bald Eagle, acting as medicine man, made a number of prayers to the Hopi gods. Some dirt was smeared on our foreheads, and we were pronounced full-fledged members of the Snake Clan of the Hopi tribe.

When I got a chance I spat on my finger and tested the dirt streak. It came off, I'm happy to say. I'd hate to think what Mrs. Glass would have said if we'd had to go across the country with those smears on our foreheads.

Since yesterday was the longest day of the year, or just a few days after the longest day, it wasn't dark yet by the time we had been adopted. We stayed and watched the Indians get ready for the dances. This was strictly a business affair, and they charged admission. First they picked a spot of open ground near the camp and made a big circle of stakes. They tied ropes around these, leaving one spot for an entrance. In the center of the circle they built several piles of sticks for bonfires, as practically all of their dances are around a fire. Rather than having to feed one fire in between dances, they had several they could light. The preparations for one were unusual.

Several of the braves dug a deep hole in the ground about eighteen inches in diameter. Shortly before the people were expected, they put several twenty-five-pound blocks of ice in the hole. They stuffed newspapers around the ice to act as insulation and on top they put a flat pan upside down. The pan was just the right size to fit in the hole but big enough to allow a fire to be built on top of it.

"When we light the fire, it burns and melts the ice. Then the fire sinks slowly into the earth and disappears." Chief Bald Eagle waved his hand. "Powerful medicine. Fools everybody."

"Is that an old tribal secret?" I asked.

"A special secret of the Snake Clan," he said. "Very powerful medicine."

As soon as it got fairly dark people began to arrive in numbers. A few rough seats had been made out of planks and adobe blocks, but most of the spectators stood. The admission charge was fifty cents, but as members of the tribe we got in free. Mr. and Mrs. Glass were guests, too, but the clan didn't miss anyone else. They were real businessmen. Sleeping Turtle was feeling a little better, and she and her mother had set up a little stand with silver and turquoise jewelery and all sorts of souvenirs for sale. They did a thriving business before the dance began. It was announced by Chief Bald Eagle that there would be a charge for taking pictures.

The Indians did a number of dances. In some the dancers were dressed like birds with great feathered wings. They also did a fire dance, a horse dance, and a snake dance. Bald Eagle and another Indian played the Indian drums and chanted in a peculiar singsong way. That was the only music. The firelight, and the odd singing, and the wild dancing seemed strange and unreal, and shivers ran up and down my spine.

For several of the dances they invited the spectators to join in. Midge and I both did, as well as a number of other children. It was fun, dancing around the fire in a sort of shuffle. Of course Midge and I, being bona fide Indians, were probably much better than the other outsiders.

The disappearing-fire dance was saved for last. Bald Eagle gave quite a spiel about the magic of the dance causing the fire to be swallowed by the earth. It was quite impressive, and if I hadn't known the secret I would have been baffled.

After the dances were over, we said good-by to our new relatives and went on back to the motel. They were going one way the next morning and we were going the other.

"Wait until I tell everyone back at school that I'm a real honest-to-goodness Indian," Midge said. "And I can show them my ring to prove it."

"Take good care of that ring, it's a nice one," Mrs. Glass said. "I was pricing some of this silver and turquoise Indian jewelry at several places today, and it's not cheap. Chief Bald Eagle gave us some valuable gifts."

"I think he could afford it," Mr. Glass said. "They won seven hundred and fifty dollars on the float, they sold quite a bit of jewelry, and they must have made seventy-five dollars at least at the dances."

"They are shrewd business people," Mrs. Glass agreed.

"Shrewd is too mild," Mr. Glass said. "I've always heard it's father who pays. You three got valuable presents. Do you know what I got? I got charged a dollar and a half for taking pictures of my own daughter!"

Monday, June 28th—Grand Canyon Village, Arizona

We are staying at the Bright Angel Lodge on the edge of the Grand Canyon. This is our second day. Tomorrow we are going on east into New Mexico.

The Grand Canyon dwarfs anything I've ever seen. You could turn the Swiss Alps upside down in it and practically lose them. One thing is certain, the snow would be gone in no time because the Canyon is hot!

I've got a whole mess of circulars, post cards, and booklets about the Grand Canyon, giving all sorts of details about how long it is, how wide, and how deep. I'm not going to put that all down here in my journal, but I suppose I should put a good deal in my finished travel book.

The fact that interested me most was that the Canyon is about seven to ten million years old. According to the little pamphlet I read, as you go down into the Canyon, you pass through all the different layers of the earth's past history, with fossils of the life that existed at different periods. The top layer was more than a million years old when erosion by water and wind first began to form the Canyon. The next lower layer is Coconino sandstone, which is still older. I saw a piece of this in the museum, and it had fossilized footprints of lizards in it. The different layers show traces of various kinds of life down to the last layer. This is a hard black rock that, according to the Park Service naturalist, is among the oldest exposed rocks on earth. It is probably more than two billion years old. It shows no sign that life existed then.

Rocks and fossils are very interesting to me. One of the naturalists of the National Park Service showed slides and gave a talk about the history of the Grand Canyon last night. It was so interesting that for a few hours I decided to study fossils and geology when I go to college.

But that was just temporary, and I guess I'll stick to my original idea of being a naturalist. Live animals are more interesting than dead ones. Also, it's a lot easier to say you're going to be a naturalist than a paleontologist. You'd have to explain what the word meant to two-thirds of the people you met, and imagine trying to spell it.

The last two days have been very peaceful, especially today. Mr. Glass said he wanted to spend a quiet, relaxed day with no excitement, and he got just what he wanted. Not that seeing the Grand Canyon isn't exciting, because it is one of the greatest sights in the world. But it's been there for about seven to ten million years, and nothing really exciting happens to it from one day to the next, like an earthquake or a blizzard. I guess they have some violent snowstorms in the winter, and the north rim is closed, but this is June.

We drove up here yesterday from Herman's Gulch. It

128

wasn't a very long drive, and we were here at the lodge in time for lunch. We spent the afternoon looking at the Canyon from various spots, and last night we went to the illustrated lecture that I mentioned. We visited the Hopi Indian house near the hotel. Midge and I told several Indians that we had been adopted into the tribe, but they didn't seem much impressed. Chief Bald Eagle should have given us some sort of an identification card, or the tribe should have a secret handshake. They haven't got their tribe set up to operate smoothly like organizations such as the Elks, the Moose, the Masons, and the Boy Scouts. These particular Hopis obviously haven't heard that we are bona fide members yet. They'll probably get a smoke signal to-morrow after we're gone.

Last night we had a soda before we went to our cabin, and Mr. Glass said he hoped nothing exciting would happen today.

"I just want to lounge around, take a few color slides, get my hair cut, eat, and be lazy. I don't want to adopt any Indians, parakeets, monkeys, or be adopted by them. There's a bus in the morning that goes to Hermit's Rest and you children can take that if you will endeavor not to fall in the Canyon. I think it leaves at nine-thirty. As for me, I'm just going to yawn and go back to sleep at nine-thirty."

I guess he did exactly what he said he would, because I didn't see him at all this morning. I got up about six-thirty and went outside. There are piñon, juniper, and dwarf pine all around the cabins. The woods are full of birds—jays, nuthatches, chickadees, robins, flickers, and hairy woodpeckers. I also saw some rabbits and dozens of chipmunks. The naturalist last night said there were mule deer, coyotes, gray foxes, and raccoons but I didn't see any. I doubt if they come very close to the cabins.

Midge got up about half an hour after I did, and we went over to the coffee shop for breakfast. You'd think people out here had never seen an Indian instead of being surrounded by them, the way they looked at Midge and me. I suppose our features don't look Indian even though we are copper-colored. I look a little mottled, and maybe the waitress thought I had some horrible disease, the way she stayed away from our table. I was starved, too.

Mrs. Glass came into the coffee shop as we were leaving. She didn't want to go on the bus trip to Hermit's Rest, so at nine-thirty Midge and I and a whole busload of other sight-seers piled into the bus and drove off. The bus stopped at Trail View, Pima Point, and Hopi Point. The whole drive was along the rim, and we got a wonderful view of the Canyon. The end point of the trip was at Hermit's Rest, which is a cliff house made out of big boulders.

We met a boy on the bus named Charlie Toretti. He lives in Illinois and is on a trip with his grandfather and grandmother. They had been to Yellowstone National Park, and firecrackers are sold in Wyoming. He had a whole package, which I tried to buy. He didn't want to sell them, but I managed to talk him out of six. We aren't going to Wyoming, which is a shame, because I'm getting discouraged about our chances of ever finding any fireworks.

We got back to the lodge about noon, and all of us had lunch together. Mr. Glass said he had slept until ten-thirty, and then after eating breakfast he had taken pictures. Mrs. Glass had spent the morning hunting wildflowers.

After lunch Mr. Glass went off to the photo shop while Mrs. Glass went to the post office for stamps.

"I feel deserted," Midge complained. "At home when they dug a ditch along the road in front of the house, my mother fussed and warned me about it for days until it was filled in. Now here I am on the edge of a mile-deep canyon, and they don't seem to care a rap. Why, Mom didn't even warn me to be careful or tell you to take care of me."

"Maybe we ought to do something dangerous then," I suggested.

"Like what?"

I couldn't think of anything except to fall in the Canyon, and I had no intention of doing that. "We could shoot off a firecracker in the Canyon," I said. "It might make a big noise."

"It'll probably make just a little pop," Midge said. "With all that space the noise will just get lost, but let's do it anyhow."

We decided to walk a short distance down the West Rim

Trail, which goes along the Canyon rim for about a mile from the lodge.

Midge wanted to change to her sneakers, which were in the station wagon, so she had to go back to the cabin, find the car keys, and unlock the car. While she was gone, a boy about eleven or twelve years old came out of the main lodge twirling a rope. He was a chubby kid and was really dressed for the Wild West. He was wearing brown cowboy boots with high heels, an embroidered shirt with leather cuffs, blue jeans, a belt with a big silver buckle, a neckerchief, and a big cowboy hat with the side brim turned up.

Strapped to his hip was what looked like a real six-shooter. I don't think even Arizona had ever seen anything like him except on television. He had a long rope and was trying to spin a loop, but he wasn't too successful.

"Do you know how to spin a rope?" he asked.

"No, I don't."

"I don't either," he said, "and I don't seem to be learning very fast."

He didn't need to tell me that. I took the rope and tried to spin it but I didn't do much better. "I think spinning ropes are usually short ones," I told him. "Then you don't have this big coil on the end to worry about. Unless you keep turning it, the rope will get all twisted."

"Well, I'm not going to cut my rope in two," he said. "Then it would be too short for roping steers."

"Are you expecting to rope steers?"

"You never can tell in these parts, pardner," he said, grinning.

"Where'd you buy the outfit?" I asked.

"Hoboken, New Jersey," he said. "They got the best Western store in the country there."

We got to talking, and it turned out that he came from Hoboken, New Jersey. He was an odd sort of kid, a natural clown. He had a round good-natured face and a bubbly high-pitched giggle that made me want to laugh with him. Everything I said or he said, he turned into some sort of a joke. The only thing he was serious about was that Western outfit he was wearing. He thought it was beautiful, and he wasn't wearing it as a joke. I saw some fancy costumes at the rodeo in Herman's Gulch, but none that could touch his. The real cowboys who entered the roping and hog-tying contests had worn ordinary blue jeans and blue shirts, but I didn't tell this boy that. After all, he'd seen more TV than I had, and so he was more of an expert on the West than I was.

"This is Terry Sylvester, Midge," I told her when she got back. "Terry, this is Midge Glass. She's from New Jersey too."

"Howdy, pardner," Terry said. "Where you mavericks headin'?"

"We're off to blow up the Canyon."

"Good idea," Terry said. "Mind if I string along?"

"It's all right with me," I said. "We'll be gone half an hour or so. We're going down the West Rim Trail a little way."

"I was down there this morning," he said. "I think I can find the trail again. Wait until I leave a note for my mother. She's in the beauty parlor."

He went toward a nearby cabin. Midge turned to me and raised her eyebrows.

"Did this character fall on his head in the Canyon, or is there a masquerade ball somewhere?"

"Neither. He's just a lonesome cowboy from Hoboken."

Terry was back in a minute, and we started down the trail. We hadn't gone far when we found a spot with a guardrail right on the edge of the Canyon and no one around. We lined up at the rail. I lighted the firecracker and tossed it out into space. It was a big cracker, but Midge was right. The noise seemed to get lost and was dwarfed by the Canyon.

"The walls still seem solid enough," Midge said.

"Set off a nuclear blast next time," Terry advised.

"I hope the fall-out kills that bug that is biting me," Midge said, trying to slap a spot between her shoulder blades.

I lighted a second firecracker and tossed it straight up in the air. It exploded before it got back down to our level. This one was much better, and I thought I heard an echo.

"Hey! I dropped the keys!" Midge shouted.

"What keys?" I asked. I knew, but I hoped I was wrong.

"The car keys," she said. "I was carrying them in my hand after getting my sneakers. Now what will I do?"

"We could drop you after them," Terry said. "That's what my pop would probably do with me if I lost our car keys."

"Is it the only set?" I asked.

"I don't know. Mom was driving when we got here, and I found them on her dresser. Maybe Dad's got another set. I'd rather not have to find out."

"If you were going to get scared and drop something, why didn't you do it on the first firecracker?" Terry asked. "You weren't so close to the edge then."

"I wasn't scared!" Midge said scornfully. "And I wasn't

very close to the edge either time. The keys were on a little loop of chain hooked over my finger. That bug was biting me, and I tried to brush it off. The keys came off my finger."

"It's not a straight drop here," I said. "Maybe they didn't fall all the way."

"That's right," Terry said with a grin. "They might be only a half or even a quarter of a mile down."

The rail looked solid, but no rail looks solid enough to me on the edge of something as deep as the Grand Canyon. I had Midge and Terry hold my belt, and I leaned between the top and middle rails and looked down. About ten feet below us was a ledge, and there on the edge of the ledge were the keys.

"That does us a lot of good," Midge said bitterly. "No one is going down there after them."

"We need a fish line," Terry said.

"Maybe your rope will do."

We didn't have any fishhooks, so we tried a big wad of gum on the end of Terry's rope. The rope was a little too stiff, and we couldn't seem to maneuver it around to touch the gum against the keys.

"Hey, I've got a paper clip in my pocket," Midge said suddenly.

While Terry and I were getting the paper clip bent into a hook, Midge began having troubles with the bug again, or one like it. She jumped around, trying to hit the middle of her back.

"That thing has crawled down inside my blouse, and it's driving me crazy," she said. "I'm going in back of those bushes and take off my blouse and get rid of it."

The bushes were about ten feet away. Midge disappeared behind them, and we began fishing for the keys. I was doing the fishing, and I didn't care for leaning out between those rails at all. I tied a loop of the rope around my stomach and then around the rail. That still left enough rope to let me reach the keys. I was maneuvering our wire hook around when suddenly I heard a woman's voice.

"What on earth are you doing?" she asked. "That's terribly dangerous."

"We lost some car keys over the edge," Terry explained. "They're on a ledge about ten feet down."

"What are you trying to do with the rope?"

"The girl who dropped the keys is on the other end," Terry said.

I wish I could have seen the expression on her face, but I had the keys almost hooked and didn't dare turn around. Terry told us later that he had one foot braced against the rail and was pretending to be pulling the rope with all his might. Of course he was pulling against the part tied to the rail. He can say almost anything with a straight face, and I suppose the woman thought anyone crazy enough to wear a costume like his would be crazy enough to lower a girl over the edge. She gave a surprised squeak followed by a dismal "Oh my!"

She turned and hurried back along the path, but I didn't know that, because just then I hooked the keys.

"Got 'em!" I said, pulling the rope up.

"Quick, Midge, she's coming back!" Terry said.

Midge came out from behind the bushes, and I handed her the keys. She was still tucking her blouse into her skirt when two women came hurrying around the curve. They were timid-looking women, probably in their sixties. The one in the lead, a tall woman with straight white hair, put her hand to her mouth, gave a weak gasp, and wilted. She leaned against the other, shorter woman.

"Thank heavens, you're safe," she said.

"She's been safe all along," Terry said. "We had the end of the rope tied to the rail."

"Please don't do anything like that again, children," the short woman said.

"We won't need to," Midge said. "I'm going to hold on to the keys this time."

"I think you'd better go back to the lodge and find your parents," the first woman said. "I'm sure they wouldn't approve of your doing anything like that."

We were headed back to the lodge anyhow, so we took their advice. They were still standing near the rail the last we saw of them, shaking their heads in amazement. I'll bet they will talk about us longer than they talk about the Grand Canyon.

"How many more firecrackers do you have?" Terry asked as we walked down the trail.

"Four."

"How about selling me two?"

I shook my head. "You'd probably set them off in the dining room and get us all in trouble. Besides, I want to keep them."

He kept arguing and making offers all the way back, finally getting up to thirty-five cents apiece. I wouldn't sell. We arrived at the lodge and went to the soda fountain. Terry ordered a Coke, and Midge and I ordered sodas. He was served first and had finished before we got ours.

"Trade you a horned toad for two firecrackers," Terry said.

"Horned toad? I'd like to see a horned toad," Midge said.

"Have you really got one?" I asked.

"Four of them."

"I'll bet," Midge said.

"All right," Terry said. "Pay for my Coke, and I'll go get them. If I really have them, I don't have to pay you back."

"And if you don't have four, you have to pay for my soda," Midge said.

"Shake," Terry said, holding out his hand and sliding off the stool.

Our sodas arrived, and we began eating them. Just as we were finishing, Terry came back carrying a box about three feet long and a foot wide. It had wire panels in all four sides and in the top. We looked inside, and there were four horned toads about five to six inches long, lying perfectly

still on a layer of sand in the bottom of the box. They had two large horns or spines in the center of their heads and a row of three smaller horns on each temple. There were pointed scales all over their bodies and tails.

"They look vicious!" Midge said. "I'd hate to have one of them bite me."

"They won't," Terry said. "They lie perfectly still when you pick them up. Sometimes they try to stick you with those horns, but they can't even do that."

A man who was standing at the cashier's counter came over to look at them. He was a pleasant-faced man with white hair.

"Those are Pacific horned toads, aren't they?" he asked. "Did you get them in California?"

"My cousin in San Diego gave them to me while we were there," Terry said.

"Horned toads are really lizards," the man told us. "The ones you see most often are the Texas variety. They are a bit shorter or stubbier than these. I believe these are hardier, though. If you take care of them, they'll live a long time. They have to have plenty of sunlight and warmth."

"I had the cage outside in the sun all day," Terry said. "I bought some meal worms at a pet store, but I'm about out of them now. It's keeping me busy trying to catch ants and grasshoppers and things like that. That's why I'm willing to trade you one for only two firecrackers. They're worth a lot more."

"Are you sure they're harmless?" Midge asked.

"They just look dangerous; they're not at all," the man said. "There's one variety that can squirt a tiny stream of blood from their eyes. Just what that is supposed to accomplish I don't know, but even that is harmless. Some varieties will puff up when you touch them; others sort of flatten out and pretend they're dead. Don't be misled when they lie still, because they are very fast when they want to be."

We left the soda fountain and were walking by the beauty parlor when one of the hotel employees came by with a cartful of paper and junk. On top of it was an old bird cage.

"Are you going to throw that away?" Terry asked.

"I certainly am," the man said. "A guest left it behind. I guess the bird died. I'll probably find the bird in a bureau drawer or some crazy place. One time a guest checked out and left a radiator from a car in his room."

Terry picked the cage off the pile of trash. It was bent and battered, but it was still in one piece.

"That would be perfect for one toad," Terry said.

"He could keep Amos company," Midge said. "Amos has been looking sort of droopy lately. Why don't you trade with him, Hank?"

I could have pointed out that she was recommending that I trade my firecrackers for company for her parakeet, but I didn't. I'd never seen a horned toad before, myself, and I figured that I'd be a lot more interested in it than Amos would be.

"All right," I said, producing two firecrackers.

"It's a deal, pardner," Terry said. He put the box down, took my two firecrackers with his left hand, and shook hands with his right.

Then he unhooked one of the wire lids. Very carefully, he reached inside and picked up one of the toads, taking hold of it just back of the head. It didn't stir, and neither did any of the others.

"Always hold onto it tight," Terry said. "That man was right, they can look like they're asleep, and then all of a sudden—zip! They're gone!"

The toad remained motionless while Terry put it in the bird cage. "There you are," he said. "I hope you enjoy your new home, Andy."

"Andy?" Midge asked.

"Andrew Jackson," Terry said. "I named them all after presidents of the United States. That's Abraham Lincoln, the one in the corner is John Quincy Adams, and this one at this end is Grover Cleveland."

142

"How did you pick which president to name them after?" Midge asked.

"They look like the presidents they're named for."

I'll admit that I don't know much about horned toads, and Terry may be an expert, but a horned toad is a horned toad when it comes to looks. The only way you could tell one of them from the others was by size. The one he had called Grover Cleveland was the largest.

"I suppose that one does look a little like Lincoln," Midge said doubtfully. "But this one like John Quincy Adams? Not a bit!"

I had my doubts if either of them had any idea what any of the four presidents looked like except Lincoln. Just then I saw a fly land on the wall, and I moved over to catch it for Andrew Jackson.

"You have to look at their profiles," Terry said. "Then you can see the resemblance."

"Let me see."

I didn't see what happened as I was concentrating on the fly, but Midge must have opened the box so she could pick up John Quincy and look at his profile. She didn't get the chance.

"Look out!" Terry warned.

It was too late. Two of the three lizards were out of the box like brown streaks. Just at that minute the door to the beauty parlor opened, and a woman came out. One horned toad went flashing past her, and the other turned in the opposite direction and went scooting down the hall.

Terry went racing down the hall after that one, leaving Midge and me to get the one in the beauty parlor. That Terry is a quick thinker.

You would have thought that poor toad was a mouse from the fuss that was made. There were only three customers and two operators in the shop, but from the screaming you would have sworn there were twenty. One woman was under a dryer, and she almost knocked her head off getting out from under the hood and jumping up on her chair. A second customer sat there half-paralyzed for a minute. Then she caught sight of the horned toad as Midge chased him toward me. She opened her mouth, gave a funny little gasp, and then was silent. She was trying to scream but couldn't. All of a sudden her scream came out full blast. It was a shame she wasn't out by the Canyon. I'd like to have heard the echo from the north rim.

One operator went running out in the hall, bellowing for help, and the other one grabbed a broom. She kept screaming, "Where is it?" swinging her broom back and forth. She was a husky-looking woman and from her wild-eyed look I wasn't sure she could tell me from a horned toad, so I kept well out of her way.

The third customer, a stocky, gray-haired woman, was the only sensible one in the place. She was having her hair shampooed and was deserted right in the middle of the shampoo by the broom-swinger. She wiped her eyes, sat up, and looked around blearily.

"Don't be so hysterical," she said. "A horned toad is

144

harmless. If you'll quit acting like idiots, these children will catch it if you don't scare it to death first."

She got up and helped Midge and me. We finally trapped him in one corner and the woman turned an empty waste-paper basket upside down and stuck it over him. Then she lifted up the edge of the basket; I slid my hand under and grabbed him. I was not sure whether I had Grover Cleveland or Abraham Lincoln, and I didn't care. No one in the beauty parlor cared either as long as we got out fast. As I walked toward the door they all shrank away from me as though I had scarlet fever. Since I look so blotchy, I'm not sure whether they were avoiding me or the toad.

A big crowd had gathered outside in the corridor, and more people were running toward us. I looked around but couldn't see Terry any place.

"What's going on?" a man asked me as I came through the door.

I was holding Grover in my right hand so I simply put him in my trousers' right pocket. I kept a good grip on him, though. My mother always says that it looks sloppy to walk around with your hands in your pockets and is bad manners to keep them there when you are talking to someone, especially an adult. I figured this was an emergency.

The one beauty operator who had rushed out was giving a garbled account to some man as they hurried toward us. He looked important enough to be manager, but I doubt if he knew how to manage that problem. If you had believed what the woman was saying, Grover had become triplets, and all three had grown into monsters.

"Psst!" Midge said. "Terry's down by the door."

"What's the trouble?" the manager asked.

"Nothing serious, I guess," I said. I ducked through the crowd after Midge, and we hurried away. Terry slipped through the door, and we were right behind him. He had his wire box in one hand and the bird cage in the other. We kept going until we found a nice quiet spot with no one around.

"It was getting awfully crowded in there," Terry said. "Horned toads don't like big crowds."

"We got ours," I said. "How'd you make out?"

"He ran down the corridor like a flash and then stopped all of a sudden and let me catch him."

I had a little trouble getting Grover Cleveland out of my pocket, and his horns ripped a couple of small holes in it, but we managed. The minute he got back in the wire box he flattened out on the bottom and pretended to be fast asleep. I knew he wasn't, though; he was resting up for another dash when the time came. I looked at Andrew Jackson in that battered bird cage and had my doubts. I could picture him dashing around inside the station wagon, which was filled to the window level with baggage and odds and ends. Midge and I would be trying to catch him, and if Mrs. Glass was anything like those women in the beauty parlor she'd be half out the window, screaming in fright. I didn't try to imagine what Mr. Glass would be saying or doing.

Midge stood looking at the cage, and I could tell she was thinking the same thing. She looked up at me and raised one eyebrow. Then she shook her head.

"Daddy's a wonderful father but he'll only go along so far. Then he explodes. He was trying to get me to throw away the pine cones this morning because there was so little room."

"It's just asking for trouble," I said. "I'd like to keep him, but I guess not."

"If you're trying to back out of the trade, nothing doing," Terry said.

"You can keep the firecrackers," I said. "It's just that we haven't room for him."

"Why don't you try to sell or trade him to someone else?" Terry suggested. "If you can't, I'll take him back. I'd rather get rid of another one, though. I spend all my time catching bugs."

"That's what my Dad says," Midge said. "The minute you have a family you have to spend most of your time supporting it."

Terry went on back to his cabin with his cage. Midge and I started to take Andrew Jackson back to the car and changed our minds. Instead we walked toward the Hopi House. We'd been there before, but it was a good place to meet people our age, and we decided the quicker we could make a trade the better.

When we got there, there weren't any likely prospects around. Two women and one man were wandering about, and there were several younger couples, but none of them looked like the horned-toad type. We were about to go back to the hotel when Midge noticed a man some distance away, sitting on a small camp stool, busily painting. His easel was half-facing the Indian House.

"Let's go see what he's painting," Midge suggested.

We walked to within a few feet of the artist. He wasn't painting the Hopi Indian House as we expected. In fact his painting had only a faint resemblance to anything I could see. It was a landscape, but the sky and clouds looked strange to me. There were a few scraggly bushes and one half-dead tree. They were the same variety as those along

the edge of the Grand Canyon but certainly the sickest-looking specimens available. Midge and I stood a few feet behind him, not saying a word. Suddenly he turned around.

"Do you like it?" he asked.

He was a young man with a little red beard that was as scraggly as the bushes on his canvas. His eyes were large, brown, and looked as though they might pop out and hit us.

"Hank is the artist," Midge said. "Ask him."

"Do you paint?" he asked.

"A little," I admitted. I do get good marks in art.

"He's a wonderful painter," Midge said. "Last summer he painted a beautiful sign on the end of a barn and some marvelous flowers on the backs of some turtles we had."

"The surfaces he paints are original, I'll have to admit that," the artist said. "Well, young man, how do you like my canvas?"

I didn't think it was anything outstanding, but I didn't want to hurt his feelings.

"The trees and bushes look pretty scraggly," I said. "But I guess that is the way you meant them."

"I meant it to be a much more desolate scene than what you see here," he admitted. "I was going to call it 'Edge of Desolation.' But it's not going too well. I never have been able to paint large scenes. A small segment with detail is more my line."

Midge moved to one side, and he saw the bird cage I was carrying.

149

"Is that a horned toad?"

"Uh-huh, his name is Andy Jackson," Midge said.

"Wonderful!" the artist said. "I'd like to paint him. And the name Andy Jackson would be perfect for the canvas. Will you rent him to me as a model?"

"We're leaving tomorrow early," I said. "We'll sell him cheap, though."

"He'd have to be awfully cheap," the artist said. "Tell you what I'll do. I'll give you this canvas for him."

I looked at Midge, and she shrugged her shoulders. We didn't want the canvas much, but at least it wouldn't get loose and run around causing trouble.

"All right," I said.

"I won't sign it, because it isn't completely finished, and I'm not too proud of it," he said. "What do I feed this beast, and what can I do with him when I've finished?"

"You feed him bugs, and you can turn him loose when you don't want him any more."

He had another canvas with him which he promptly put on the easel and began painting. Andy Jackson in his cage was placed on the sand a few feet in front of him. We waited a few minutes but we could see this was going to take some time so we said good-by and started back to the cabin.

"What will we do with this thing?" I asked. "It's going to take up some space. Maybe not as much as a bird cage, but some."

"I think I can put it flat right in with my clothes in that blue suitcase," Midge said. "When we get back home someone will buy it as a painting by a Grand Canyon artist. If not, I'll keep it for my museum."

No one was at the cabin when we arrived. Midge wrapped the painting in newspaper and put it in the bottom of her suitcase. It fitted perfectly and took up scarcely any room. A few minutes later Mr. Glass appeared, having taken enough colored pictures of the Grand Canyon to satisfy six camera bugs. Mrs. Glass had four scraggly plants, which she carefully hid in the back of the station wagon before coming into the cabin. Both of them were grubby and hot, so they each took a shower, and we all went over to the restaurant for a nice leisurely dinner.

"Well, this has been a quiet lovely day," Mr. Glass said, leaning back in his chair while he was waiting for a second cup of coffee. "No crises, no alarms, and no excitement."

"It has been a lovely day," Mrs. Glass agreed. "Although I'll admit that I had a few qualms just before getting back to the cabin. I was walking behind a group who were telling some dreadful tale about two boys lowering their sister over the edge of the Canyon wall on a rope. I began to think we were foolhardy to let Midge and Henry go off alone."

"That story encourages me greatly," Mr. Glass said happily. "I had my hair cut this afternoon, and while I was in the barber shop there was a great to-do about some children releasing some poisonous snakes or lizards in the hotel and several women being bitten."

"I think that's dreadful," Mrs. Glass said. "What's encouraging about it?"

"Both stories prove that things happen to other people too," Mr. Glass said. "There's not some peculiar aura or cloud following us alone. I was beginning to think there was, and I didn't know how to face the rest of the trip."

I had a notion to tell him that what those two stories proved was how two simple little stories could be stretched out of all shape by the time a few people had retold them. I decided not to, however. Midge and I just looked at each other. Sometimes it's best to protect adults by not giving them too many details.

Tuesday, June 29th—Taos, New Mexico

We are in New Mexico now. I haven't seen a sign of any firecrackers for sale.

We covered a lot of territory today and saw a lot of things. We got up about five o'clock and were all packed and ready to go by five-thirty. Mrs. Glass has a little electric pot, and she made some instant coffee for everyone, and we had some fruit to eat. It was three hours before we found a place to have breakfast.

We forgot all about our painting until Mr. Glass began loading the station wagon. It's a good thing it was out of sight in Midge's suitcase because for some reason or other things didn't fit so well when Mr. Glass packed this morning. Maybe he was sleepy. He got the luggage carrier on top loaded full and started to put the remainder of our gear inside. Then he saw the four plants Mrs. Glass had collected.

"What are these?" he asked.

"Plants," said Mrs. Glass. "I'm going to take them home."

"You're going to take *those* all the way to New Jersey?" Mr. Glass asked in a voice that said he thought she was insane.

"I picked the smallest ones I could find," Mrs. Glass said.

"Picking flowers is illegal in national parks," Mr. Glass announced happily, "and digging up plants is probably an even worse offense."

"I had the permission of the park naturalist," Mrs. Glass said. "I also have a slip that will let me get by any inspection stations at state borders."

This disappointed him, I could see. He looked at the four plants in disgust. "They look pretty scrawny and flea-bitten to me right now. After ten days or more in the car, they'll look like last year's dead weeds. How are you going to water them?"

"At the motel at night," Mrs. Glass said. "These are semidesert plants anyhow and can take a great deal of heat and dryness. They'll get home all right."

"Maybe they will, but I'm not sure we will, because we are fast approaching the point that I will have to drive with packages on my lap. It's considered good practice if the driver at least has enough room to move his arms."

We finally found enough space for the plants and were about to drive off when Midge discovered that one of her bags of pine cones was still sitting beside the cabin steps. She had picked up another bunch of cones at the Grand Canyon and had them in a separate paper sack. Since she wanted to keep the pine cones from each place identified, we had all sorts of separate little packages. Mr. Glass found a small space and wedged the paper bag in that. It split open and dumped the cones all over. I thought he was going to blow up, but he didn't. We got the door shut and were on our way. After we had gone about twenty miles, Mr. Glass finally spoke. "Get some sort of bag or satchel or sack for those pine cones tomorrow in Taos, Margaret. If they are still in those paper bags when we leave Taos, I'll throw them all in a trash can."

We drove along the south rim of the Grand Canyon and out the eastern end of the park. At Cameron, we turned south. Cameron was nothing but a service station and lunchroom. Although it was so early when we went by that the restaurant wasn't open, it was already hot. That service station was the driest and most deserted-looking place I've ever seen. We were really in the desert.

We drove on through Holbrook, Arizona, and detoured off the highway to go through the Petrified Forest. We had a late breakfast at the lunch counter at the National Monument headquarters, and Midge bought a piece of petrified wood for her museum.

Just to the north of the highway as we left the Petrified Forest was the Painted Desert. We drove through that. It was beautiful, but it doesn't take long to see what there is to see, and by noon we were well into New Mexico. We didn't stop in Albuquerque except to get gasoline. We did stop in Santa Fe for several hours, and we all would have liked to stay longer. It's an interesting old town with a square in the center that looks like part of Mexico or possibly Spain. You can go through the old Spanish Governor's Palace which is very interesting, and there is a museum.

One of the most interesting places was a shop where they sold all sorts of souvenirs. They had dozens upon dozens of different kinds of rocks which were polished into beautiful stones. You could buy earrings, rings, pins, tie clips, and necklaces made of every color and shade you can think of. You could also buy small pebbles or big slabs of rock, cut or uncut, polished or unpolished, and make your own jewelry. Hunting for rocks seems to be a popular hobby in New Mexico and other parts of the West. People go around with little hammers that look like masons' hammers. They break open every rock they can find, hoping it will be some unusual color. Confirmed rock hunters are called "rock hounds." While we were in the store a man came in with a great big rock weighing about fifty pounds. It was an unusual color of purple quartz. He and the store owner got quite excited about it. I followed them into the back room, where there were all types of saws for cutting rocks in two and a huge vibrating machine which was used for polishing. It takes a lot of equipment to be a real rock hound.

I bought a tie clasp with a stone made of petrified wood. There are all different colors of petrified wood, but this one was brown agate. Midge bought a lot of jewelry to give as Christmas presents, and so did her mother.

There was a paperback book on rocks which I bought.

I'm going to study it, and maybe I'll turn into a rock hound. There isn't much rock around Uncle Al's home in New Jersey except red shale and pieces of old cement sidewalks or foundations. I don't think either one would polish up to look like anything, but Mr. Glass said there are many different kinds of stones and minerals in northern New Jersey.

We had to leave Santa Fe before we were ready to go, because Mrs. Glass's cousin in Taos was expecting us. Mrs. Glass has relatives all over the West. I asked how her family got so scattered, and Mr. Glass said he suspected it was because they couldn't bear to be close to one another. She says that isn't true; they just happened to move here and there.

We got to Taos, New Mexico, about six-thirty. Mrs. Manton, Mrs. Glass's cousin, is a woman about fifty-five or sixty years old who used to be the fashion editor of a women's magazine and has retired. She still writes articles now and then. Her house is very old but comfortable. It has adobe walls about two feet thick, which she says help keep it cool in the middle of the summer. The floors are tile, and the walls are painted. My room was a small white room with nothing in it except a low bed and a bureau. The walls were painted white, and there was no decoration except one painting of a burro on one wall. It sounds plain, but I liked it very much.

Mrs. Manton took us out to dinner at a place that specializes in Mexican food. I didn't know what I was eating half the time, and I very nearly burned my tongue off, but I enjoyed it.

Taos has a square in the center of town just as Santa Fe does, and after dinner we walked around looking at the shops. I guess Taos lives off the tourist trade, and the shops were all open to catch any tourist that wandered by. There was an art exhibit in one building, and Mrs. Manton and Mrs. Glass stopped to look at it. Most of the art was modern, or surrealist, or whatever you call paintings that make no sense. Midge claimed most of them were hung upside down, but that wasn't true, because the artists had signed them, and you could tell which side belonged up. Each canvas was tagged with a price, and the prices weren't low. Some were marked three hundred dollars, and the cheapest in the place was twenty dollars.

"Can anyone enter a painting?" Midge asked the woman who seemed to be in charge.

"Certainly. The exhibit opened yesterday, but the judging will not take place until tomorrow morning at eleven."

"What does it cost to enter a painting?" I asked.

"Nothing to enter one, but all canvases entered must be offered for sale, and if we sell them, we receive twenty per cent commission."

"I'll bring mine in early in the morning," Midge said. "What time do you open?"

"Nine-thirty."

"Are you crazy?" I asked, when the woman went over

to talk to two possible customers. "That painting is a landscape. It would look silly with all this modern stuff."

"We can doctor it up," Midge said. "There's a store right down the street. Come on, we'll get a brush and some paint."

Midge and I said we were going on to look at other shops and then hurried to the art supply store. We bought two brushes and five tubes of oil paint. Mrs. Glass was still at the art exhibit when we returned, but Mr. Glass had gone on to a curio shop. We joined him, and eventually Mrs. Glass and Mrs. Manton caught up with us. It was still early when we got back to Mrs. Manton's house. The adults sat down and started talking about nothing, the way adults do, so Midge and I moved out to what Mrs. Manton called the "patio room."

"I'll get the painting, and we can fix it up tonight," Midge said. "There may not be time in the morning."

"A painter is supposed to have natural daylight," I objected, "not a fuzzy light from a sixty-watt bulb."

"We'll just call it 'The Sixty-Watt Scene,'" Midge said. "That'll puzzle everybody. They'll spend days trying to figure out what it means."

Midge had picked out bright orange, a bright green, some dark purple, white, and turquoise. I tried to think of something I could paint with those colors. It wasn't easy.

"You're supposed to have some idea what you want to

paint and then you mix or buy the colors you need," I told her. "What can I paint with that dark purple except maybe an eggplant?"

"Perfect," Midge said. "Put a nice big eggplant in this corner. Nobody will have the slightest idea what it means, so they'll be very impressed."

I painted the eggplant in the upper left-hand corner of the canvas. This put it up in the sky, next to a wisp of a cloud. Since I had one vegetable, I decided a second one would fit in, so below the eggplant I painted a good-sized carrot with a bushy top. Midge was very pleased with the result.

"Now we need something else silly on the right side, lower down," she said, standing back and looking at the painting as though she were an art critic, which I guess she is.

"This is not a pure white, it's eggshell," I said, looking at the tube of paint. "How about an egg?"

"That's a good idea," she said. "Balance it right here on this little mountain peak."

I painted the egg, and I have to admit the painting did look more interesting than it had before. It certainly had more color. I hadn't used any of the turquoise, and I was trying to think of something that color when a spider ran across the floor. I'd never seen a turquoise spider, but then I'd never seen an egg balanced on a mountain peak. I painted two spiders climbing up toward the egg and showed the results to Midge.

"Sheer genius!" she said. "That gives it class and a real deep message."

"What is it?" I asked. "I'm not tuned in."

"The art critics will think of the meaning," she said. "All you have to do is to agree with them. Now we need a signature."

I certainly didn't want to put my initials on that thing, so I signed "RG" in the lower right-hand corner for Reed and Glass. Midge was pleased with that too. Last summer I had a research firm called "Henry Reed, Inc." and toward the end of the summer I made Midge a full partner and changed the name to "Reed and Glass Enterprises."

"We'll win a prize," Midge said.

"I'll bet you an ice cream cone we don't."

We put the canvas aside to dry, and then I started writing in this journal. I really should put down some more travel information about both Santa Fe and Taos, but I'm too tired. I think I'll go to bed.

Wednesday, June 30th—Taos, New Mexico

Today has been a very successful day even though I haven't found any firecrackers. I met several Indians, visited an Indian pueblo, and Midge and I made some money.

As soon as breakfast was over we walked downtown with our painting. Midge wanted to show it to her mother and Mrs. Manton, but I put my foot down. It was such a silly-looking thing, and I thought the whole idea of exhibiting it was so crazy that I didn't want anyone to know that we were connected with it. We didn't say a word but slipped it out of the house without anyone seeing. On the way to the art gallery, we argued about what price to put on it. I said ten dollars, but Midge wanted to make it fifty. We finally split the difference and agreed to sell it for thirty.

The art gallery wasn't open, but we saw the woman inside, and we knocked on the door. She took the painting, held it off at arm's length, and examined it very seriously.

"Quite interesting, quite interesting," she said judiciously. "An unusual conception."

We didn't stay to discuss the painting, because we

wouldn't have been able to keep our faces straight. We told her the price was thirty dollars and then hurried back to Mrs. Manton's.

During the morning we all drove out to the Mission of St. Francis, which is about four miles from Taos. It is a beautiful church built by the Franciscans more than two hundred years ago. Then we went to the Pueblo de Taos which is an ancient Indian village that is still inhabited. It is a jumble of adobe buildings four and five stories high. The streets are very narrow and winding, and the Indians climb from one level to another by ladders. We had to get permission to visit from the governor of the pueblo, who was an Indian chief.

After lunch Midge and I wanted to visit Kit Carson's house, which is right in Taos. Mrs. Glass didn't want to see that, so she and Mrs. Manton didn't come with us but went shopping.

Kit Carson lived in the house from 1843 to 1868. It was furnished exactly the way it had been when he lived there, with the exception of one room, which has a collection of guns, saddles, and other items used in the old West. We spent quite a while there and then wandered around the plaza for a while. It was about four in the afternoon when we got back to Mrs. Manton's house. It was a relief to get inside those thick adobe walls, because it was blistering hot in the sun. Mrs. Glass and Mrs. Manton were still out somewhere.

"They must not mind the heat," I said to Mr. Glass.

"Women will endure almost any hardship while shopping," Mr. Glass replied. "If there had just been a big store or some sort of shopping center at the end of the trail, the women of pioneer days would have slogged across the great plains and the deserts without a second thought. And woe to the redskin who got in their way."

I have been shopping with my mother a number of times, and Mr. Glass is right. My feet hurt and I get tired all over, but my mother keeps right on going. The odd thing is that it doesn't seem to make any difference if she buys anything or not. It's just hunting for something to buy or not buy that she seems to like.

About half an hour after we got back, Mrs. Glass and Mrs. Manton arrived. They were talking excitedly as they paused in the little foyer.

"They got a rare bargain," Mr. Glass said with a grin. "They outsmarted everyone else and got the best buy in the store."

When they came into the room, Mrs. Manton was carrying a big flat square package wrapped in brown paper. Mrs. Glass had one small box about a foot square and a shopping bag. Mr. Glass looked at her packages and then at Mrs. Manton's and gave a slight sigh. I knew exactly what he was thinking. He was wondering where to put two more packages in the station wagon and at the same time feeling relieved that Mrs. Manton had the biggest package.

"I got a lovely piece of Indian pottery," Mrs. Glass said,

putting down her package. "It's black, a rare glaze that's the secret of one Indian family."

She put her shopping bag down and began opening the square box. Mrs. Manton sat down in a nearby chair and leaned her package against her chair. When Mrs. Glass had her package open, she removed a low round vase from it and held it up for us to see. It was a dull black and very nicely shaped.

"Isn't it lovely?" she asked.

"It is," Mr. Glass agreed. "I hope it's also unbreakable so it will stand a chance of getting home."

She put the vase back and opened her shopping bag. From it she pulled two leather handbags and two belts.

"Real leather, hand-tooled. A bag for Midge and me and a belt for each of you two."

Mine was a very nice belt with a silver buckle. I liked it, and of course I thanked her. Mr. Glass's belt was less a cowboy belt and more like a dress belt, but it was still very nice. He thanked her and naturally, after receiving a gift, he couldn't very well start complaining about where she was going to put the two bags she bought for herself and Midge.

"And I've saved the real prize until last. Look what I got at the art exhibit!" Mrs. Glass got up and took the big square package from Mrs. Manton.

"You bought that?" Mr. Glass said, getting slightly red-faced. I could see him trying to hold in the explosion. He couldn't blow up while he was a guest in someone's house. It was like putting a cork in a foaming soda bottle, though.

"This won honorable mention at the exhibit," Mrs. Glass said happily. "One of the judges wanted to give it first prize. It has just the right colors for our family room."

She removed the wrapper and proudly held up the painting. There was our landscape with the vegetables and spiders. Mr. Glass wasn't the only one trying to hold in an explosion. Midge gave a snort, and I had to look out the window.

"It's a fascinating painting," Mrs. Glass said. "The style and subject matter are both unique."

"The style of the painting fascinated me," Mrs. Manton said. "A good part of it is traditional landscape, expertly done but in rather muted colors. Then the painter seems to have changed his personality. Look at the bold brilliant colors of that carrot and the almost primitive verve of the eggplant."

I didn't care for having my style called primitive when I've had two years of art lessons but I kept quiet. Mr. Glass looked at the painting weakly and said, "That's a bold, vivid carrot, I'll grant you that."

"I think there's deep significance in this canvas," Mrs. Glass said. "I'd love to know what the artist had in mind. I think the vegetables express some inner hunger."

"It's a wonderful painting," Midge said. "I like it a lot, and I think the artist must have had something really important in mind when he painted it. Do you mind if

Henry and I run down to the plaza to get an ice cream cone? He owes me one."

"Go ahead," Mrs. Glass said. "Get a small one, though. I don't want you to say you aren't hungry when it's dinnertime."

We hurried out and practically ran to the art exhibit. We collected twenty-four dollars, our thirty less the commission of twenty per cent. Then to our surprise we got two dollars for honorable mention. The woman was busy, which was a good thing, because I didn't want to answer a lot of questions about who had painted what. We hadn't been told of any rule that two people couldn't work on one painting, and neither Midge nor I had claimed that I had done the entire canvas. In fact we hadn't claimed anything, and I figured it was just as well to leave matters where they were. We went up the street and got our ice cream cone. Midge insisted I pay for it out of my pocket, saying the painting proceeds belonged to the firm.

"Sooner or later we've got to tell your mother," I said. "If you don't, it'll slip out sometime. It's always best to tell things like this voluntarily; then they can't do much but admit that it's a joke on them."

"Let's make it later," Midge said. "After we get back to New Jersey. Then both Dad and Mom will have more of a sense of humor about the whole trip. You know, I think the firm of Reed and Glass has a real future in modern art."

Friday, July 2nd—Denver, Colorado

The Wild West has certainly tamed down. We're practically out of the West now and still no firecrackers. I'm getting pretty disgusted.

We left Taos early yesterday morning and got to Denver easily by the middle of the afternoon. We stayed at the Brown Palace Hotel, which is a wonderful place. I think it is my favorite hotel. I'm going to recommend it in my travel book. It has very good rooms, the people that run it are friendly, the food in the restaurants is good, and there is always something interesting happening. Take this afternoon and evening, for example; in the short time we've been here, a lot has happened.

There are two buildings to the hotel, the old part and a new annex. I suppose the new part is all right, but my recommendation is to stay in the old part. It's a lot more interesting.

The hotel is about nine stories high, and it has a big hollow well in the center. You step out of your room onto what amounts to a balcony that looks down into this hollow well. You can stand at the iron railing and look down at the lobby on the ground floor. From the top floors the people walking around look like pygmies. If you look across you can see the doors to all the rooms on the opposite sides. The hotel would make a wonderful setting for an exciting adventure story. I can imagine a spy trying to sneak into a room to steal some valuable plans and the hero seeing him from across the big well. They could have an exciting chase around and around that center court and up and down from one floor to another. In fact something like that happened to Midge and me only it wasn't spies we were chasing.

I guess I'd better start at the beginning. Right now I'm sitting in the lobby while we are waiting for our car to be brought around. I'll probably have to finish this in the station wagon, so if my writing is scribbly, that is the reason.

As I said, we got here yesterday afternoon. We saw a little bit of Denver and then we went to a restaurant and had a wonderful steak. Next we went up to the top of the First National Bank. It has an observation roof, and you can see for miles and miles. Denver is a mile high to begin with, so you are really up in the air. We watched the sun set over the mountains. It was a beautiful sunset, the kind that if an artist painted it, no one would believe him.

This morning Mr. Glass had one call to make, but he said he expected to be ready to leave by noon. Mrs. Glass went to the beauty parlor, warning Midge and me not to go more than a block from the hotel and to be careful about crossing streets, and not to spend our money foolishly, and not to fill up on a lot of candy and junk before lunch. There were three or four other things we weren't supposed to do—the standard things that parents always tell you. I think there must be a printed list of such warnings that all adults use.

"And don't buy anything big that will take up space," she said as she got in the elevator. "Your father is getting very sensitive about how we've loaded down the station wagon."

Every night when we stop, Midge takes Amos, the parakeet, into her hotel or motel room. Usually she lets him out of the cage for a few minutes to give him exercise. I know exactly how he must feel, because riding all day in the station wagon is about the same thing for us as his being cooped up in that cage.

For some reason Midge didn't let Amos out last night, so she decided to let him take his exercise this morning. She let him out in her room, and then we went outside in the corridor to look down at the lobby. We decided it wouldn't be safe to leave the floor until Amos was back in his cage, because the maid might come in to clean the room, open the window, and let Amos escape.

I could have stood at the rail looking down at the lobby for hours. It's fun watching people hurrying around, shaking hands, greeting each other, and picking up their mail, especially when you are watching from seven stories up.

About ten o'clock a whole herd of noisy characters, all wearing broad-brimmed hats, seemed to flow into the

171

lobby from all sides. They took over the place, slapping each other on the back and shouting halfway across the lobby. Most of them lighted cigars, and soon a blue cloud began to float up toward us.

"A big storm just blew in from Texas," Midge said. "Do you suppose there's a cattle drive on?"

"I don't think they're from Texas, in spite of the Stetsons," I said. "Texans are supposed to be tall and lean."

"You're about forty years behind the times," Midge said. "Don't pay any attention to what you see on television and even less to what the Texans tell you. We went through Texas on the way out. Most of them ride around in air-conditioned Cadillacs instead of on horses. My father says the sagging waistline has replaced the sagging gun belt in Texas. Do you know why they never take off these Stetsons unless they absolutely have to? It isn't that they don't know any better—they all have big bald spots."

Midge was being funny, but she was very nearly right. Most of this group had sizable stomachs, and they looked prosperous and very well fed. They weren't all from Texas, though. I remembered a sign in the lobby which said there was a convention of Highway Contractors of the Southwestern States or something like that. Probably some of the Stetson-wearers were from Arizona, New Mexico, and Colorado. Apparently they had been at a meeting, and this was the intermission before the next session.

Suddenly we heard a shout, "Howdy, pardners, how's Andy Jackson?"

We looked up and there on the opposite side of the well on the floor above was Terry Sylvester. He was wearing his cowboy outfit, but he'd left his rope in his room. Except for his gun he looked exactly like all the men down below in the lobby. We waved at him and told him to come down to where we were. He headed for the stairs and a minute later was standing beside us.

"This is great," he said. "How long are you going to be here?"

He was disappointed when we told him that we were leaving at noon. I guess it gets lonesome taking a long vacation with no company at all except your parents and some horned toads.

"How's Andy Jackson doing?" he asked again.

"We got rid of him," I told him. "We traded him off to a painter."

"And in Taos we sold the painting for twenty-four dollars," Midge said. "We made out all right."

"I didn't," Terry said. "One firecracker fizzled. Just a measly little old bang not half as loud as a paper bag makes when you break it."

"How about the other one?" I asked.

"It made enough noise, but I had bad luck with it. There were a lot of people around the swimming pool at the motel, and I decided to scare them. I lit it but just then an enormous truck roared by, and everybody thought the bang was a backfire. No one was scared enough to fall in the pool."

I felt sorry for Terry. He wasn't complaining or asking for anything, but since we had made out so much better on the trade than he had, I decided to give him another firecracker. I had only two left and I didn't see much chance of getting any more, so it was a tough decision.

I was gone only a minute, but by the time I had returned with the firecracker, the corridor was filled with big-hatted Texans. They were all over like flies and making twice as much noise.

"I'm splitting my supply with you," I said to Terry, handing him the firecracker.

"Thanks," Terry said. "Mighty fair of you, pardner."

He looked down in the lobby, and Midge and I looked down, too. We were all thinking the same thing, I know. The longer you looked down at the lobby with all those people milling around, the more the idea of dropping something grew on you.

"I suppose they'd put us all in jail," Terry said.

At that minute one of the Texas invaders stopped beside us, looked at the firecracker in Terry's hand and asked, "Sonny, is that a firecracker?"

"Yep."

"I'll give you a dollar for it," he said, pulling out his wallet.

Terry shook his head. "It's the only one I've got."

"Two dollars."

"Sold," Terry said.

The man paid Terry two dollars and went on down the corridor with the firecracker.

"I know what I'm going to do when I get through school," Midge said. "I'm going to sell firecrackers in Texas."

We stood watching the lobby for several minutes, and then Terry suggested we all go down to the drugstore.

"Let me put Amos back in his cage first," Midge said.

We turned around. There was the door to her room wide open. The maid had gone by us while we were talking to Terry, or else she had come from the other end of the corridor.

"Quick," Midge said. "He's liable to fly out."

We raced down the corridor and into the room. The maid was making up the bed and she looked at us as though we were lunatics.

"Where's Amos?" Midge asked, looking around.

"Amos?" the maid asked. "There's no one here unless he's under the bed."

"Amos wouldn't be under the bed," Midge said, looking up near the ceiling. "He's a bird."

We looked all over, including the closet and the bathroom, but Amos was nowhere in sight. The windows were all closed, so there was no doubt where he had gone. We hurried outside and started looking at the far end of the corridor. It took only a minute, because there aren't too many places, except behind a fire extinguisher or two, where a bird can hide in a hotel corridor. Amos was not there. He could have gone only one place—out to the big hollow well above the lobby.

"That is just ducky," Midge said. "He might just as well be loose in Grand Central Station."

We looked around sort of helplessly and hopelessly. There were so many floors, and it was such a huge place that there seemed little chance of ever spotting one tiny blue parakeet. To make matters worse, more of the big

Texans had appeared, and they were scattered all over. Some were walking along the corridors to and from their rooms, and others were standing by the rail talking and looking down at the lobby. I guess they enjoyed watching the people too. Trying to spot Midge's bird in all that forest of hats looked impossible. What's more, Amos could have flown down or up to any of the other floors and disappeared down their corridors.

We were about to give up when suddenly Terry spotted him, sitting on the rail two floors down. He seemed to be watching the lobby, just as everyone else was doing. We all ran for the stairs.

"We'll come up on him from both sides," Midge said. "You do the catching, Hank. You've got a way with birds and animals."

I didn't have the right way, it seemed. We were within three feet of him when he flew across the open well to the next floor above.

After the first two attempts, we quit running up and down the stairs and used the elevators. Even so, in a short time we began to get tired and discouraged. Amos could fly directly across the big well, and it was a simple matter for him to fly from one floor to another. We had to go all the way around, either to the elevator or the stairs. We walked or ran a hundred feet while he flew ten.

After ten minutes or so, the situation improved a little. The men with their big hats began to wander downstairs again. They slowly congregated in the lobby in a big milling herd. I suppose the next meeting or session of their convention was about to begin.

On our ninth or tenth unsuccessful attempt, Amos flew to the seventh floor. We decided on a different strategy. Midge went to the sixth, Terry went to the eighth, and I went after Amos. By this time the corridors were practically deserted. I stayed close to the wall and got to within eight or ten feet of Amos. Then I dropped to my knees and started crawling toward him. I was inching forward very slowly when the door to a room opposite me opened, and a man came out. He was the big man who had paid two dollars for Terry's firecracker. Beside him was a short stubby man in a light blue shirt. Both of them were

smoking huge cigars. They walked to the railing, looked down for a minute, and then the bigger man reached in his pocket. Amos seemed to be watching too, so I inched closer. I put my hand up toward the rail very slowly and was within a few inches of Amos when, out of the corner of my eye, I saw the man toss something into the big open well. As it fell it left a thin trail of smoke. I froze, waiting for the explosion.

According to television, two cowboys could shoot each other dead on the street, and no one would bother to go to the door to see what the noise was about. Maybe gun shots have a different sound from firecrackers, but, as I mentioned before, I believe the Wild West has tamed down. That firecracker certainly created a commotion. Of course, everything was in its favor. It was a loud one to begin with, and it went off under perfect conditions. It was about halfway down to the lobby when it exploded. That big hollow well with the corridors stretching off from it magnified the noise, and the sound echoed back and forth until you would have thought a dozen firecrackers had exploded together.

For two or three seconds there was complete silence. Even the hum of people talking stopped completely. Only three people in the entire hotel were not surprised—the two men on the opposite side of the well, and me. Even Amos was petrified. They couldn't have timed that firecracker better. My hand was within a few inches of the parakeet, and it was a simple matter to reach out and grab him. I stood up and, as I did, the people in the lobby below began to recover from their shock, and the place practically blew up a second time. I've never heard such a fuss over a simple little thing like a firecracker. Several women screamed, men shouted, and everyone did his best to make as much noise as possible. I don't know whether they thought someone had been murdered or the hotel had blown apart.

The two men opposite me began laughing like hyenas. The big man was doubled over the rail, really enjoying his joke, when the shorter one yanked at his arm and said something. Then they both turned like a couple of cowards and ducked back into their room.

Small pieces of firecracker began floating down and heads began to look upward. By this time Terry and Midge had recovered from their surprise and were looking over the railing. I knew what would happen. It was near enough to the Fourth of July that people would think of firecrackers. When they looked up and saw three kids peering down, they were certain to blame one of us. I wanted to stay around and watch the fun, but it wasn't safe. I moved back so that no one could see me from below and motioned to Midge to come and for Terry to get out of sight.

Terry, instead of going back to his room, came down to our floor. He appeared about the same time as Midge, and we all went into Midge's room.

"What happened?" Midge asked.

"That big gunman from Texas who bought Terry's fire-cracker tossed it down the well."

"I wanted to do that," Terry said, "but I was afraid I'd get in trouble. What are we in here for? Let's go back and see the fun."

"And get blamed," I added. "The man who threw it, and another man with him, ducked out."

"At least that one wasn't a dud," Terry said. "I'll bet there would have been even more commotion if we'd sold him a horned toad and he'd tossed that over. I wonder if he'd be interested?"

We put Amos back in his cage and were looking at a fold-out series of pictures of Denver when Mr. and Mrs. Glass arrived.

We introduced Terry to Mr. and Mrs. Glass. "Nice to meet you, Terry," Mr. Glass said. "I'm sorry, but this is going to be a short acquaintance. I've checked out, and the car has been ordered. Everybody close his suitcase and check to see that he has everything."

"What was all that fuss in the lobby, Ernie?" Mrs. Glass asked, as she looked in the closet to see that Midge hadn't left anything.

"There was some sort of explosion," Mr. Glass said. "I suppose it was a prank of one of the conventioneers. I don't know why it is, but some conventions seem to be attended by overgrown boys."

"Conventions of chemists are always serious affairs,"

Mrs. Glass said. "They hide the women's shoes and things like that."

"The chemists who attended the convention weren't responsible for that," Mr. Glass said, "just their dogs and their children."

He stopped suddenly and looked at Midge and me. "Henry, you've been trying unsuccessfully to buy firecrackers everywhere we've been. How did you make out in Denver?"

"They don't sell them here," I said.

"You didn't by any chance set off a firecracker here in the hotel, did you?"

"No sir," I said.

"I wasn't accusing you," Mr. Glass said. "I just remember something your uncle said about things having a habit of happening when you were around."

"We've been as quiet as mice," Midge said. "We heard the explosion, though. In fact if it hadn't been for the noise we might never have caught Amos. He was having a ball, flying back and forth in that big open space above the lobby."

"Amos was loose out there?" Mrs. Glass asked. "Whatever on earth for?"

"He got out," Midge said.

"Hmm," said Mr. Glass. "Perhaps that noise was a shotgun being fired. Bird shot probably. Someone probably objected to having a parakeet flying over his head. As you say, you two were quiet as mice."

Friday night, July 2nd—Gopher Springs, Kansas

I'm really disgusted. Here it is two days before the Fourth of July, and I haven't seen a sign of a firecracker. All I have to celebrate Independence Day with is the one lonely firecracker I got from the boy who had been to Wyoming. I'm beginning to think Wyoming is the only patriotic state in the West or maybe even the nation. There is certainly space enough out here for all the fire-crackers in the world to blow up without anyone even noticing, but you can't buy any.

I tried to think of some good reason why we ought to go from Denver to New Jersey via Wyoming, but I couldn't. I doubt if Mr. Glass would have listened any-how. He seems anxious to get home now. He has plenty of vacation left, but the car is getting so full he's afraid to stay on the road much longer.

About fifty miles outside Denver we came to a little town with a junk shop. It had a big sign, "Antiques and Junque." Mr. Glass must have missed the sign, or I'm certain he would never have stopped at the gas station across the road. He checked the tires, paid for his gas, and started to get behind the wheel, when he noticed Mrs.

Glass and Midge were missing. He settled back, thinking they had gone to the rest room.

"They went across the street to that antique shop," I told him.

"Antique shop! Why didn't you warn me, Henry? Sometimes you can forestall these things by turning on the motor and pretending you're ready to go whether you are or not."

"My dad did that one time before they'd taken the hose from the gas tank," I told Mr. Glass. "He practically pulled the gas pump off its base."

We drove across the street and parked in front of the shop.

"I doubt if even my wife can find anything in that place," Mr. Glass said, looking at the dirty windows.

The words were hardly out of his mouth when Mrs. Glass appeared, carrying a cardboard box. Midge was right behind her, carrying a glass lamp.

"I bought the loveliest lamp," Mrs. Glass said. "I was afraid to have it mailed. If it ever got broken you could never replace it."

"That's good," Mr. Glass said, looking at the lamp. "Might I ask where the people in this car are going to sit?"

"Oh, I can repack things so there will be plenty of room," Mrs. Glass said.

She repacked some things and managed to find a place for the lamp. I don't know that I would call what was left "plenty of room," but we all managed to get in.

"Sooner or later we are going to have to start throwing people overboard," Mr. Glass said. "Have you two children ever seen that painting of the Russians in a sleigh being chased across the snow-covered steppes by wolves?"

"I have," I told him.

"Do you remember what the woman in the back of the sleigh was doing?"

"She was about to toss a baby to the wolves," I said.

"What a horrible idea," Midge said. "Why would she do a thing like that?"

"I always assumed she was sacrificing her baby to the wolves to allow those in the sleigh time to escape. Now I realize that in my thoughts I've wronged those people. They weren't that callous after all. They just wanted room!"

I don't know what he meant, because we haven't seen a wolf on the entire trip. Midge seemed to know, because she started to giggle. I think Mrs. Glass was annoyed for some reason or other.

We are staying at a nice new motel, but it has no swimming pool. We certainly could use one. In case you've never been in Kansas in July, it's hot. They ought to make it a state law that every motel in Kansas has to have a swimming pool. Tomorrow we are going on to Hansonville, Kansas. I certainly hope we find a pool there.

Saturday, July 3rd—Hansonville, Kansas

We are in a little town in Kansas called Hansonville. It's located on the southern border near Oklahoma. It's dry, dusty, and hot. No one driving through would ever notice it, and the only reason they would ever stop would be to buy gas or to spend the night at the motel. The people of Hansonville are very friendly, which is good, because we are going to be here several days. Mr. Glass went to school here when he was a boy. This is the first time he has been back since his family moved away about the time he finished the eighth grade.

I like Kansas, and I think it would be a wonderful place to live if they would just change their silly laws about firecrackers. Here it is the day before Independence Day, and you can't buy a firecracker anyplace.

It has really been hot driving today. All day long we sweltered, and the only thing that kept Midge and me from melting away to grease spots was the hope of finding a swimming pool at the motel tonight. About ten miles out of Hansonville we saw a big sign which said, "Stay at the Motel Sunflower at Hansonville—Air-conditioned

Rooms—Air-conditioned Lounge and Dining Room—New Swimming Pool."

"Is that where we're staying?" Midge asked.

"It is," Mr. Glass said. "When I lived here, there was an old ramshackle hotel called the Grand Hotel. It was about to fall down then, and I imagine it has since. I hope the Sunflower Motel will be slightly more modern, but I have no faith whatever in signs."

The sign told the truth, and the Sunflower Motel is a very attractive brick motel on the edge of town. The rooms are air-conditioned and so is the dining room. There is a swimming pool, but there is one hitch. There isn't any water in it. It's so new it isn't finished.

The swimming pool is made of steel. I thought that pools were always made of concrete, but on this trip we've been swimming in several made of steel. Right now this one looks like an enormous tank sitting up above a big hole in the ground. When Midge saw it wasn't finished she gave a yowl that they must have heard in Oklahoma. I felt just as disappointed, but I didn't yowl.

We all went into the office while Mr. Glass registered. Mr. Glass looked at the man behind the desk several times and then said, "Aren't you Jim Murray?"

"That's right."

"I went to school with you through the eighth grade."

Mr. Murray looked at the register and said, "Fuzzy-top Glass! It's been a long time, hasn't it. Good to see you!"

Midge started to giggle at the idea of her father having the nickname of "Fuzzy-top." He's two-thirds bald now. It's hard to imagine your parents or the parents of your friends as kids with silly nicknames, but they were once human, too.

Mr. Glass and Mr. Murray spent some minutes talking about what became of this or that classmate, or how they fooled Miss Somebody-or-other who was once their teacher. From the conversation, I'm surprised they didn't get kicked out of school every week. They'd never get away with as much today. I guess they were more lenient with kids when our parents were young. Sometime or another Mr. Glass must have done some studying, because he is considered to be a brilliant research chemist now.

By the time we were settled in our rooms, it was dinnertime, so we went to the dining room. About halfway through the meal Mr. Murray came over and joined us.

"You're in the doghouse with the younger element," Mr. Glass told him. "They were looking forward to a swim."

"I'm in the doghouse with everyone over that pool," Mr. Murray said sadly. He looked like my beagle Agony does when he's lost a rabbit trail. "I doubt if anyone in the county will speak to me after Monday."

"Why?"

"I promised it would be ready for the Fourth of July.

188

You may have noticed that the American Legion and the Volunteer Fire Company are setting up that field across the way for a big celebration. Tomorrow is Sunday so the celebration will be Monday, the fifth. Several months ago I promised the pool would be ready and all children could swim free. There isn't any place to swim within fifteen miles, and I think the children were looking forward to swimming more than they were to anything else in the celebration—even the fireworks display. You know it gets hot here in Kansas—much hotter than it did when we were young, in my opinion. I'd like to take a swim myself."

"What's the holdup?" Mr. Glass asked. "Why isn't it finished?"

"Do you remember Bud Turney? We used to call him 'Goof.'"

"Sure, sandy-haired, stringy, with a long nose."

"That's the boy. Well, he's done all right. He has a welding engineering company over in Coffeyville. He builds a lot of oil storage tanks down through Oklahoma and Texas. Things were slow for him this spring, and when he heard that I planned to build a pool, he wanted to build it out of steel. He gave me a good price—he's my brother-in-law—so I told him to go ahead. I bulldozed the hole, laid the pipe that goes under the pool to the center drain, and got everything set. He laid those beams across the hole, brought the steel in, and fabricated the tank."

"It looks practically completed," Mr. Glass said. "What's the snag?"

"There were two cranes working on the bridge over Gannet's Creek. Goof arranged for them to lower the tank into place after he was finished. Then all he would have to do was weld in the bottom connection and hook up a few pipes. But he goofed. He pulled two men off to work on a rush oil-tank job and delayed this work for a week. The two cranes had to move over to the other end of the county, and we can't get them back for at least three weeks. I'm what you might call 'high and dry.'"

"Do you mean the only thing that keeps that pool from being finished is getting it down into that hole?"

"Looks simple, doesn't it?" Mr. Murray asked bitterly. "I thought so too, for a while. Believe me, that is no simple operation. That is a big tank—fifty-two feet long and twenty-eight feet wide. It weighs tons!"

"Can't you just yank those beams out and let it drop?" Mr. Glass asked. "It's sitting directly over where you want it, isn't it?"

"It is," Mr. Murray agreed, "but it's not that easy. In the first place nothing can yank those beams out while the weight of the tank is on them. Secondly, if it isn't lowered gently and evenly, you will twist the tank and break the welds."

"Lower it on the beams and remove them later."

"That sounds possible, but it isn't. I have the ground all

smoothed out underneath the tank, ready for it. I would have to dig trenches across to allow for the beams. Then the beams would be down in the ground, and I'd either have to leave them there and pay for them or do a major excavating job to get them out. It would add more than a thousand dollars to my cost."

"This does seem to be a problem," Mr. Glass admitted. "Aren't there any other cranes?"

Mr. Murray shook his head mournfully. "Not any heavy enough. I thought of bringing in every wrecker within miles. When we calculated how much that tank weighs, we decided that all of them together wouldn't budge it."

He got up to go over to speak to some other diners. He certainly was sad about his pool, but he wasn't any sadder than I was. I wanted to swim. I was still thinking about it when our dessert came. I had ice cream. I was watching it melt slowly when I happened to think of the Hopi Indian fire dance and how the melting ice had made the fire disappear.

"I know how to lower the tank into the hole," I said to Midge.

Midge thinks I can do anything. Of course she's usually right, but sometimes she has so much confidence in what I say that it puts me on the spot. This was one of those times.

"Henry can get the tank lowered," she announced to her father, not even bothering to ask how I would do it.

"That so?" Mr. Glass asked, between bites of pie. I could see he wasn't taking her too seriously.

"Mr. Murray!" Midge called. "Henry's got a plan!"

Mr. Murray had left the other table and was walking toward the cashier's counter. He didn't hear her, and I was just as glad.

"Don't be in such a hurry," I told Midge. "We ought to talk this idea over first."

"Do you really have an idea that will work?"

"I think so."

"Then what is there to talk over? Time's a-wastin'."

"Well, it's really an old Hopi tribal secret," I said. "Do you remember that disappearing-fire trick? It's based on that. Maybe we shouldn't say anything."

"I don't see why not," Midge said. "Just don't mention the Hopi trick, and no one will ever connect Hopi fire dances with a swimming pool in Kansas. Besides, it can't be such an old secret. The Hopis never saw any ice before the white man invented refrigeration."

"What are you two muttering about?" Mrs. Glass asked.

"Henry's plan to lower the tank," Midge said. "It's wonderful, and I think we ought to tell Mr. Murray."

"What is it?" Mr. Glass asked.

"I don't understand it exactly," Midge said, "but it's got something to do with ice."

"Why couldn't you raise the tank a little, build some

piers of ice under it, pull the beams out, and let the tank melt down into the hole?" I asked.

Mr. Glass paused with his coffee cup halfway to his mouth. He froze that way for a minute and then he said, "Henry, give up the idea of being a naturalist and chasing bugs. The country needs engineers like you. Hey, Jim! Come over here! Henry's solved the problem!"

Mr. Murray came over and Mr. Glass explained my idea. As he listened he got more and more excited.

"I'll need about two truckloads of ice. I can get Bert Simpson to go over to the ice plant in Coffeyville. Maybe they'll have another truck. If not, I'll dig up one someplace."

In about an hour there were at least fifty people working around the pool. I think the entire volunteer fire company turned out to help. They got a number of heavy construction jacks and jacked the beams up about six inches. Everything was ready by the time the trucks arrived with the ice. By nine o'clock they had built eight square piles of ice blocks. The real excitement came when they slowly let the tank down on the columns of ice. I don't know what people thought would happen. Maybe they thought the ice would be crushed, but nothing happened at all. The tank simply sat on the ice. All the onlookers and workers stood looking at it with pleased smiles until suddenly Mr. Murray came to life.

"Don't let down now. We've got to yank those beams

out of there fast before the ice melts and lets the tank
back down on them."

They put chains around the beams, hooked them to a
tractor, and in a few minutes had dragged them clear.
This left nothing between the tank and the bottom of the
hole but the ice. Mr. Murray looked worried. I know what
he was thinking. He was wondering what would happen

if the ice slipped at one end and not at the other and the tank got twisted and ruined. Nothing happened, however. Mr. Glass was the most confident one there. He said the heavy weight of the tank had pressed all the big ice cakes into one solid mass and there was little danger of the piers collapsing. He was right, I'm glad to say. By eleven o'clock the tank had dropped noticeably. Mr. Murray had men inside the tank, walking around. They kept checking on how it settled. If it didn't go down evenly they planned to put tubs of hot water over the piers that were melting too slowly. I don't think they have had to do it, but I don't know because Midge and I had to go to bed.

"It'll be hours before all that ice melts," Mr. Glass said. "There's nothing to watch, so you two might just as well go to bed."

Mr. Murray came over to shake hands with me. "Henry, you're the hero of Hansonville," he said. "You've saved the day. By tomorrow afternoon I expect to have it ready for swimming. At the celebration Monday I was supposed to make a little speech. I'd like you to be up on the stand with me, so I can tell them who deserves the credit for having the pool ready in time."

It feels good to be called the "hero of Hansonville," but it's a big responsibility. I can't get to sleep thinking about it, which is the reason I am bringing my journal up to date. It's now after twelve. I just peeked out the window, and the tank seems to be settling all right. I'd certainly feel terrible if something went wrong and I got up in the morning to find the pool was wrecked.

It isn't just the pool that worries me. If I get up on the stand with Mr. Murray I might have to make a speech.

I've never made a speech to a big crowd before, but I rather like the idea. The trouble is I don't know whether I should admit the idea wasn't really mine but belongs to the Hopi Indians, or whether I should keep quiet, as Midge says, and protect the secret of their disappearing fire. Making important decisions is a tough job.

Sunday, July 4th—Hansonville, Kansas

We are still in Hansonville at the Sunflower Motel. The pool is fine. Everything worked perfectly, but being a hero is something I can do without. All you get is responsibility and headaches. Maybe I should say backaches.

The whole town spent the day getting ready to celebrate tomorrow. I don't understand this business of postponing a holiday because it falls on Sunday. Midge asked her mother about it, and Mrs. Glass explained that it wouldn't be proper to fire off fireworks and to spend the day celebrating on Sunday since Sunday is a day of worship. That may be so, but Sunday is supposed to be a day of rest too. No one rested in Hansonville. They were all working like beavers getting ready for tomorrow. I don't see how anyone had time to go to church.

The firemen put up all sorts of stands, they built a platform for the judges, and for speeches, and they roped off areas for pony rides, races, and all sorts of games. On this side of the road they were just as busy. Sometime very early this morning they welded in the bottom connection, and by the time we went to breakfast, the pool was partly full of water. About nine o'clock, they began filling in dirt around the edges and laying a temporary walk of flagstones. Later Mr. Murray plans to put in a regular coping and a cement walk.

Mr. Glass spent the morning visiting old friends around town. Mrs. Glass stayed in her room, reading, with the air conditioning turned on full blast, and Midge and I watched all the activity across the street and at the pool. It was scorching hot, and by noon we were ready for a swim.

We were rather late eating lunch. Mr. Murray came over to our table before we had finished.

"Well, Henry, you can christen our pool whenever you're ready. I'd like you and Margaret to be the first ones to use it."

That sounded like a wonderful idea to us, so neither Midge nor I ordered any dessert. That was just a waste of a piece of cherry pie as it turned out, because Mrs. Glass wouldn't let us go in for forty-five minutes anyhow. I could digest the one hamburger I had eaten in ten minutes, but I didn't argue since I'm a guest on this trip. It was almost two-thirty when Midge and I walked out to the pool in our suits.

As I said, being a public figure has its disadvantages. There were a number of people still working, and they all stopped to watch. They had installed the diving board by this time, and someone said I ought to christen that too.

I'm not much of a diver. Midge claims that I dive in six directions at one time, which is impossible. I've never had much chance to practice diving, and I can't see too well without my glasses, so I'm always a little scared of falling off the diving board. If I hadn't been a hero I could have climbed down the ladder or at most jumped in from the edge of the pool. As it was, I had to dive in, and everybody had to watch.

I walked to the end of the board, took a deep breath, and made the best dive I could. I think it was a pretty good dive for me. I've never had such a shock as when I hit the water. It couldn't have been more than a degree or two above freezing. I had gone into the water in a fairly deep dive. I tried to flatten out and get back up to the surface and in doing that I put an awful kink in my back. I was under the surface in that ice water an hour at least. When I finally did break the surface I could hardly breathe. I think my chest muscles were frozen.

Somehow I managed to swim over to the ladder. My back hurt so that I had to climb out sideways. I still can't stand up very straight.

"How was it?" Midge asked.

"Cold," I said, when I could stop my teeth from chattering.

Everybody clapped and cheered as I climbed out, but from now on someone else can be the hero. I've learned two lessons. One is never to betray a Hopi Indian secret and the other is to stick your toe in the water before you dive.

Monday, July 5th—Hansonville, Kansas

We celebrated the Fourth of July today. It is quite a celebration the way they do it in Kansas. If it wasn't for the kink in my back, I think I would have had the best time I've ever had on the Fourth of July.

The celebration got under way about eleven o'clock this morning and lasted until now. In fact it's still going on, but we were all tired and decided to go to bed. We have to get up early in the morning and start for home.

There weren't any Ferris wheels or merry-go-rounds, or rides of that kind, but no one missed them. There were all sorts of games, races, and contests; there were stands galore where you could buy wonderful hamburgers, cake, watermelon, and food of all kinds; there was a band; there were speeches; and there was the swimming pool. Above all there was a whole town full of people who were in a good mood and wanted to have fun. They certainly did.

At eleven o'clock, the mayor got up on the band platform and informed everyone that Mr. Murray had offered the use of his motel pool for the day. Mr. Murray had to stand up and take a bow, be cheered, and make a short speech. Of course everyone knew all about the pool before the mayor said a word, but they listened as though it were news and cheered every few words. The people in Kansas are very good-natured and polite.

The mayor went on to explain the difficulties they had had in getting the pool finished and then said I had "saved the day." I was introduced as the "best engineer in Kansas." I had to stand up, and everyone cheered and clapped. I didn't have to make a speech, so I didn't say anything about the Hopis. It's a lot of fun being a hero after all. I had to stand sort of crooked because of the kink in my back that I had got diving into the pool. I suppose I looked peculiar standing up there all catawampous, but I couldn't explain why. I didn't want to in the first place, and then I didn't want anyone to think my trouble was the fault of the pool, because that wouldn't be fair to Mr. Murray.

It was a blistering hot day, and the kids didn't even wait for the mayor to finish his speech about the pool. About forty of them had arrived with their suits on under their other clothes, and in nothing flat there was a screaming horde of kids running across the road to the motel. Two of the firemen acted as lifeguards, and they had their hands full. The water in the pool went up about six inches when everyone jumped in. The guards had a rough time keeping one kid from jumping on top of another, but they managed, and there were no accidents. If the water was cold they didn't notice, or else there were so many they warmed it. I don't think water can wear out, but if it could that water would have been worn out by mid-afternoon.

Midge went in swimming three times. I went in only once because I was afraid of really fixing my back with all those kids jumping around. They thinned out about five o'clock, and I slipped in for a few minutes.

The bingo game was the biggest attraction of the celebration. I'd never seen a bingo game before. Midge says she has seen dozens of them but none as big as this or with people so interested. I guess the reason the game was such a success is that they had hundreds of wonderful prizes, some of them worth a lot of money.

At first Mrs. Glass refused to play. "It's just a modified form of gambling, and I don't approve of gambling. I don't care if churches and religious organizations do sponsor games. In principle, it's wrong."

"Just consider that you're giving them the money you pay to enter," Mr. Glass said. "As a matter of fact, you usually are, because there isn't much chance of winning. The money goes to charity or some worthy cause, so you can consider it a charitable contribution."

My mother says that children are changeable and inconsistent. Adults aren't any better. Take the Glasses on the subject of bingo for instance. They completely reversed themselves during the day. It's peculiar how it happened.

Mrs. Glass refused to play at all for some time. Mr. Glass, Midge, and I played several games during the morning, and about three o'clock in the afternoon went back to play again. Mrs. Glass wandered off by herself for a few minutes and then came back as we started our second game. She was looking rather annoyed at being left out of things. I suppose being so righteous while we were having fun was quite a strain. We had just started our second game when an old schoolmate of Mr. Glass's appeared with another man in tow. Mr. Glass had to get to his feet to shake hands, and he would have missed two numbers if I hadn't watched his card for him.

He introduced Mrs. Glass to the two men and then said, "Take my card over for a little while, will you, Hazel, while I talk to Bert?"

Mrs. Glass was in a spot. She didn't want to go into a long explanation of why she wouldn't take over the bingo card, so she swallowed her principles and sat down. She had watched us enough that she knew how to play. I suspect that, in spite of her disapproval, she was interested. At any rate, she played like a veteran. Mr. Glass wandered off with his two friends. The game had barely started as far as I was concerned when suddenly Mrs. Glass had her hand in the air and was yelling, "Bingo!" in an excited voice that you could have heard across the street at the motel.

She won a new toaster, which pleased her. "We need a new toaster," she said. "I suppose I'd be foolish not to take it, and after all it's Ernie's card."

We had paid for three cards, so she played once more.

While we were playing, Mr. Glass came back. He slipped up behind her, saw the toaster, and raised his eyebrows. I nodded, and he grinned. He left again, without her seeing him.

None of us won anything that game, but Mrs. Glass had two rows of four.

"Let's play one more," Midge said.

It didn't take much persuasion. "I suppose I should make a little larger 'contribution,' as Ernie calls it, after having won this expensive toaster," Mrs. Glass said, getting out her purse.

Everyone who won a prize got a ticket, and at ten o'clock this evening all those with tickets were entitled to enter a play-off game for the grand prize, which was a choice between a number of appliances at Gillian's Appliance Store. It really was a grand prize, too, because you could pick a refrigerator, freezer, dishwasher, washer, or dryer.

At first Mrs. Glass wasn't going to enter, but we kept urging her.

"You haven't half paid for that toaster," Mr. Glass said. "It will cost another dollar to enter, even with your qualifying ticket. You owe them that much."

"I suppose I do," Mrs. Glass said. I think she wanted someone to convince her it was her duty.

Mr. Glass bought her card for her, and she sat down without any more argument. The first four numbers on her card were in a straight line, and she got so excited she couldn't talk. Then the game dragged for what seemed ages. Every place you looked, someone had four in a row. I think she had given up hope when they called B4, which completed BINGO for her.

All she could do for several minutes was gurgle and wave her hands. I don't think they would have known she was the winner if Midge hadn't shouted, "Bingo!" for her. The person who was really surprised, however, was Mr. Glass. His face sagged, and his jaw dropped.

He mumbled something which I didn't catch and then said, "It always happens this way, always! Why some poor sucker who has been playing and hoping for years couldn't win, I don't know."

"Ernie, I've won, I've won! Do you realize what's happened?"

"I certainly do," Mr. Glass said, recovering rapidly. "Congratulations. I'll have to look up Mr. Gillian and see if I can't make some cash settlement with him."

"Cash settlement?" Mrs. Glass said indignantly. "I get my pick of appliances, and I'm going to take a freezer. I've wanted one for three years."

"Look, Hazel, we're fifteen hundred miles from home. A freezer is a sizable piece of equipment that people haul around in a truck, not in a station wagon already bursting at the seams."

"We can't go off and leave it!" Mrs. Glass said. "After the sacrifice I've made to win it."

"Sacrifice! What sacrifice?"

"My principles," Mrs. Glass said. "It wasn't easy for me to go against my life-long beliefs about gambling."

"Look, I imagine I can make some sort of arrangement that the manufacturer who makes whatever freezer you pick will deliver a similar one to New Jersey," Mr. Glass said. "It is simply out of the question to take a freezer with us, you know that."

"I suppose," Mrs. Glass said, looking very sad.

At that moment Mr. Gillian appeared and congratulated Mrs. Glass for winning. When Mr. Glass explained that we were leaving early in the morning, he was most obliging. He went downtown with us and opened up his store.

"You can have your pick of any freezer of all those along that wall," he said, waving his hand.

While Mrs. Glass looked carefully at every freezer, Mr. Glass explained that they lived in New Jersey and couldn't very well take the freezer with them.

"I imagine we can work something out," Mr. Gillian said. "I'll find out from the company who your nearest dealer is and see if he can't deliver it."

"This is the one I want," Mrs. Glass said finally, standing in front of a big upright freezer.

Mr. Gillian shook his head. "You can have that particular freezer, but you'll have to take it with you. That's a deluxe model from last year. It was a wonderful freezer but a little too expensive to sell well, and it's been discontinued. That's why it's in that line with the other lower-priced models. The chances are ten to one no dealer in your part of the country would have one left."

"Oh dear, that's the one I'd decided upon," Mrs. Glass said. She began at the end of the line again, inspecting each one.

"There's one possibility," Mr. Gillian suggested. "You could hire a U-Haul trailer."

Mrs. Glass was near enough to hear his remark. "That's a wonderful idea!" she said. "We're cramped for room anyhow."

"I think it's a miserable idea," Mr. Glass said. "I don't like to drive with a trailer, especially for fifteen hundred miles."

"You've been complaining about how crowded the station wagon is," Mrs. Glass said. "This would relieve all the congestion. Think how comfortable we'd be with all that junk moved back to a trailer."

"Think how uncomfortable I'd be with a trailerload of junk pushing me downhill and dragging on me uphill."

Mr. Glass put up a good battle, and I think he would have won if Mr. Gillian hadn't given Mrs. Glass so much encouragement. He kept telling her what a bargain the discontinued model was and how it was made of much finer material than the current models.

"You can get a trailer right down the street on the opposite corner," he said, looking at his watch. "It'll be open about another fifteen minutes. Now if that's what you decide to do, I'll get the freezer in a carton while you get the trailer. And I'll get someone to help us load it."

Midge and her mother stayed in the store while Mr. Glass and I went down to get the trailer. We were gone about fifteen minutes, and when we went back we drove around to the back door. It took Mr. Glass about six tries to get the trailer backed up to the loading platform.

"That's what I mean about trailers," he said as he got out.

The man who had waited on us at the service station came over and helped load the freezer. It was laid flat on its back on two boards and tied securely in place. It was eleven o'clock as we drove away.

"Henry, did you notice anything peculiar about that young man who helped Mr. Gillian load that freezer?" Mr. Glass asked me.

"He seemed to know more about it than Mr. Gillian did."

"Exactly my impression," Mr. Glass said. "And Mr. Gillian knew the exact hours of that service station."

"What on earth are you two talking about?" Mrs. Glass wanted to know.

"Henry knows," Mr. Glass said.

I wasn't certain, but I had a suspicion. We went around the block to get back on Main Street, and there was a big sign right across the face of the service station, "Gillian's Super Service."

"I have been had," Mr. Glass said. "I think I'll take out some insurance on the freezer and trailer and then hope all the way home that it comes disconnected going up a steep hill."

Tuesday, July 6th—En route across Missouri

Today has been the best day of the trip. I found some firecrackers! Missouri is a wonderful state!

We started about seven o'clock this morning and were

in Missouri by nine. About ten o'clock we went around a curve, and there was a gift store and novelty shop right out in the middle of nowhere. There was a huge sign saying "Fireworks."

"Daddy! There's fireworks! Henry has been looking all over for firecrackers!"

"All right," Mr. Glass said, pulling into the parking lot. "Henry has shown admirable restraint in loading us down with useless impedimenta on this safari, and he's entitled to his fling. Any space in the trailer is yours, Henry. You are limited only by the cash you might happen to have to fritter away."

It was a marvelous place. They had all kinds and sizes of firecrackers. They had cherry bombs, pinwheels, sky-rockets, roman candles, sparklers, torpedoes, snakes, whirli-gigs, and things I'd never even heard of. I spent the ten dollars I'd been saving and my half of the money we made on the painting in Taos. I probably spent a lot more than I should have, but I got the most beautiful collection of fireworks in the world. I got some real bargains too, because the woman in the shop didn't want to keep them for another year.

I had three big parcels when I finished. I put them in the trailer beside the freezer. They'll be dry and safe there, because we have a canvas tarpaulin over everything in the trailer.

Friday, July 9th—Grover's Corner, New Jersey

I'm home. I suppose that isn't correct since I'm really at the J. Alfred Harris home in Grover's Corner. He's my uncle, but it seems like home to be back with him and Aunt Mabel. I spent last summer here, and this is where I met Midge Glass. She's home too, of course, and we were both glad to get here.

The last four days have been tiresome. We've done nothing but drive all day every day since leaving Kansas. We've been on the road four days, and all four of them were hot as blazes. We were lucky, because we found motels with swimming pools every night. Even Mrs. Glass went swimming, which proves how hot it was.

The driving wasn't easy. The trailer on the back of the car slowed us down quite a bit. The first day it kept swaying back and forth, and Mr. Glass pulled into a service station and had them adjust the trailer hitch. That didn't improve matters much, and Wednesday he stopped and

213

had the trailer wheels checked for alignment. That didn't help much either, and finally he gave up and drove under fifty the rest of the way.

We had a different sort of trouble with the trailer today. Last night at the motel Mr. Glass backed up under a tree, and a branch caught the tarpaulin and ripped a hole in it near the rear end. The ripped part began flapping up and down today as we drove along, and finally quite a big hole was frayed in the canvas. We stopped twice along the Pennsylvania Turnpike and tried to tie the two sides of the rip together, but it didn't work. By the time we crossed the Delaware River, it was really flapping in the breeze again, but Mr. Glass wasn't in any mood to stop.

"It doesn't look like rain, and that tarp is shot anyhow," he said. "I'm anxious to get to the quiet and peace of my own humble abode. After four days of dragging this trailer halfway across the continent, I want to sit in a nice big easy chair in one spot for a while."

It was five-thirty when we arrived at Grover's Corner. That is exactly the right time to see everyone. I think someone was cutting grass or gardening or sitting in every yard. Of course there are only nine houses in Grover's Corner—there aren't many people. I know them all, but not as well as Midge does. I've spent one summer here, and she's lived here all her life. She had the car window open and was waving to everyone and saying hello as we went by. They all stopped whatever they were doing and came trooping to the Glasses' yard to welcome us back.

Mr. Glass stopped in the driveway, and we were hardly out of the car before a crowd gathered. My Uncle Al came up and shook hands, and Aunt Mabel kissed me.

"You made it, Ernie," Uncle Al said to Mr. Glass. "I'd have sworn it couldn't be done. I'll bet it wasn't easy."

"It wasn't dull, I'll grant you that," Mr. Glass said.

I don't know how to explain what happened next. Mr. Glass thinks it all started with the truck we passed about half a mile from Grover's Corner. There were about fifteen men in the back who had been working somewhere nearby and were being taken back to Princeton, I suppose. Possibly one of them flipped a cigarette, and it landed in the trailer. Maybe it was one of the neighbors, although Uncle Al says no one that he saw was smoking. Mr. Ainsworth was the first one to notice.

"Something's smoking in your trailer," he said, pointing.

We looked back, and a curl of blue smoke was coming up from the back end of the trailer. Mr. Glass started toward it, but he was too late. The fireworks started before he could get there.

It was a wonderful display although the pinwheels really didn't have much chance. Some of the skyrockets must have been pointing up, but I'll never know how many were wasted. The firecrackers certainly were good

ones. I never heard so much noise in such a short time in my life.

None of the neighbors knew what was happening. They disappeared even faster than they had appeared. Uncle Al said later it was good training for a missile attack, and I think some of them thought that was what had happened. Everyone vanished, and if they had bomb shelters I guess they went into them.

It didn't last long, but it was a magnificent display while it lasted. I feel badly about not having any left, but in a way I'm glad it happened. I'd have used the fireworks gradually, and they'd have lasted the rest of the summer. I know I'd have been too stingy ever to fire everything off at one time. When everything goes at once, though, it really creates quite an impression. It certainly put some zip into our homecoming.

The four of us were surprised, but after a few seconds we realized what was happening. Midge jumped up and down and screamed, she thought it was so funny, and Mr. Glass had a big grin on his face. Mrs. Glass didn't seem to appreciate the display much but she was probably worried that her freezer would be damaged. It's probably safe though, because it has that heavy box protecting it.

There were still a few scattered pops when Uncle Al poked his head out from behind a big maple tree. "Is the shooting over?" he asked.

"You can come out," Mr. Glass told him.

218

"Hey, someone knocked over Amos' cage, and he's out!" Midge said, suddenly noticing the empty cage.

"You did, with your crazy jumping," Mrs. Glass said.

We both began looking for Amos while Mr. Glass tried to explain everything. That took a little time, because one of the neighbors had been so scared she had telephoned the state police. I don't know what Mr. Glass said to them, but they didn't arrest me, although fireworks are against the law in New Jersey.

As soon as the house was unlocked, Midge got an old sheet and spread it on the lawn. We placed the cage in the center of the sheet and then moved away.

Uncle Al looked at his watch. "About seven minutes, you've been here," he said. "Nothing's happened except a fireworks display, a visit from the state police, and an escaped parakeet. That's about par, I'd say."

"I hope Amos is reasonable," Midge said. "We spent all last summer chasing a rabbit, and I don't want to spend this one chasing a parakeet."

I got my suitcase out of the station wagon and helped Mr. Glass unload some of the bundles and bags from the luggage carrier on top.

"We thank you for hauling our nephew across the country," Uncle Al said to Mr. Glass. "It's been a quiet summer here, but I dare say it will liven up a bit now. Some day soon I want to hear all about the trip."

"I've got it all written down in my journal," I said

219

as we started across the street. "Where we were, what we did, and what we saw. You can read it if you'd like."

"I'll enjoy it," Uncle Al said, "but I'd like to have Ernie's version too. You know, for a man who has been on a vacation, he doesn't look very rested."